THE PYRAMID

by the same author

THE PYRAMID

by

William Golding

FABER AND FABER
London · Boston

First published in 1967
by Faber and Faber Limited
3 Queen Square London WC1
First published in this edition 1969
Reprinted 1974 and 1978
Printed in Great Britain by
Robert MacLehose and Company Limited
Printers to the University of Glasgow

ISBN 0 571 08988 7 (Faber Paperbacks)
ISBN 0 571 08011 1 (hard bound edition)

For My Son
DAVID

"If thou be among people make for thyself love, the beginning and end of the heart."
from the INSTRUCTIONS OF PTAH-HOTEP

It was really summer, but the rain had fallen all day and was still falling. The weather can best be described by saying it was the kind reserved for church fêtes. The green leaves were being beaten off the trees by the steady downpour and were drifting about in the puddles. Now and then there would come a gust of wind so that the trees moaned and tossed their arms imploringly, though they had been rooted in our soil long enough to know better. Darkness fell early—indeed there had seemed little light all day, so that the process was slow and imperceptible. But when it was complete, the darkness was intense beyond the street lights and the rain still fell through it. I had played the piano until my head sang—pounded savagely and unavailingly at the C Minor Study of Chopin which had seemed, when Moisewitch played, to express all the width and power of my own love, my own hopeless infatuation. But Imogen was engaged to be married, that was the end.

So I lay, dry-mouthed, and endured. The only thing that pulled me out of myself every now and then was the sudden sound of blown water, dashed over the panes like gravel. Eighteen is a good time for suffering. One has all the necessary strength, and no defences. Midnight clanged from the tower of the church, and before the twelfth stroke had sounded, the three sodium lights in the Square went out. In my head, Imogen drove his green, open Lagonda across the downs, her long, reddish hair flying back from her pale face—she was only five years older than I was. I ought to have done something; and now it was too late. I stared at the invisible ceiling, and she drove; and I saw him, so secure, so old, so huge in his ownership of The *Stilbourne Advertiser*, impregnable. I heard his gnatlike voice and suddenly he was struck by lightning. I saw it branch down, there was a puff of smoke and he was gone. Somehow, the lightning had rendered Imogen insensible. I was carrying her in my arms.

I leapt up in bed, staring at the window, and clutching the counterpane to my chin. The noise had been so loud, so sharp. It had rapped the glass almost to breaking point, as if someone had used an air-gun. I had hazy thoughts of blown branches or dislodged tiles but knew it had been neither—and there it was again, rap! I huddled out of bed, my hair pricking at the strangeness, went to the window and peered down into the Square. There was another rap close by my face, so that I ducked, then peered forward; and just outside the railings that separated our cottage from the cobbles round the Square I could see a white face glimmering. I eased up the sash and immediately the wind whipped the chintz curtains in my face.

"Oliver! Oliver!"

A wild hope made my heart turn over; but it was not Imogen's voice.

"What is it?"

'Not so loud!"

The face bent down by our iron gate, opened it cautiously, then swam up the brick path and stopped under my window.

"Who is it?"

"It's me. Evie. Evie Babbacombe. Can't you see?"

"What—"

"Don't wake anybody up. Come down carefully. Dress. Oh please be quick! I'm—"

"Wait a minute."

I ducked back into the room and fumbled around for my clothes. I had seen Evie often enough, and for years; but I had never spoken to her. I had seen her sliding along the pavement on the other side of the Square with that unique walk of hers, body still, only the legs below the knees pacing past each other. I knew she worked next door, in Dr. Ewan's reception room; knew that she had a long bob of glossy black hair, and a figure that rearranged the blue and white cotton dress—knew she was the Town Crier's daughter and came from the tumbledown cottages of Chandler's Close. But of course we had never spoken. Never met. Obviously.

I tiptoed down the stairs, in the dark, avoiding the third tread, and hearing a mellow snore from my parents' bedroom. I lifted my mackintosh from its peg in the hall, then unchained, unbolted and unlocked the front door as carefully as if I had been a burglar at a safe. Evie was huddled close to the other side of it.

"You've been ages and ages!"

She was making a curious singing noise with her teeth. This close to, I could see that she had a scarf over her hair and was clutching her coat to her with both hands.

"Been as quick as I could. What d'you want?"

"Bobby Ewan's in the woods with the car. He can't move it."

Whatever vague surmises or expectations had been floating on the current of my blood vanished abruptly. Bobby Ewan was Dr. Ewan's son. We were neighbours, and I did not like him. I only envied him his boarding school, his prospective promotion to Cranwell, and most of all, his red motor bike.

"He's nothing to do with me. Why doesn't he try Henry Williams?"

"Oh dear."

She sagged a little, swaying forward against me. Perhaps behind the clouds the moon had risen; or perhaps the clouds themselves were rising. But for whatever cause, there was a diffused light now, faint, and seeming to come from everywhere at once, or be inherent in the nature of the air. By this light I could see her in more detail. Her face was very white, mouth and eyes like black plums, with straggles of hair smeared across them. Water ran on her and dripped from her. She snivelled, gripped my biceps with her fingers, bowed her head against my chest.

"My heel came off, too. What Dad'll—"

She jerked back her head in the beginnings of a sneeze and clapped both hands over her mouth. She convulsed silently. Farted.

"Pardon."

The plums glanced up at me over her hands. Under them she gave an embarrassed giggle.

"Look, Evie—what d'you want me to do?"

"Help him get the car out of the pond."

"The pond!"

"*You* know where—straight on through the woods at the top of the hill—Oh please—Olly! Nobody must know. It'ud be awful—"

"That's between him and his father—silly young ass!"

Robert was three months older than I was, and Evie, three months younger.

"You don't understand Olly—it isn't his father's car!"

"Serve him right then."

14

"Oh Oliver—I thought you would!"

She came forward, close against me. Her breasts pressed against me; and as if she could exhale it at will, I caught a whiff of scent that stopped my breath. Her coat hung wetly and there wasn't much clothing under it.

"I got to be in by midnight—"

"It's past, now."

"I know. If Dad finds out—"

For all the chill and wetness of the night, my heart had begun to go thud, thud. My arms put themselves round her. She was shivering steadily.

"All right."

She squeezed my arms.

"Oh Olly you are a real sport!"

The bottom one of her three plums lifted and gave me a cold peck. She pushed me away.

"Be quick. You could go on your bike."

"Haven't got a light. I'll run—and Evie—"

"What?"

"Shall we—I mean—we could—"

She seemed to rearrange herself—put one hand up as if she would push back her draggling hair.

" We'll have to see, won't we?"

Then she was away, hobbling through the Square and thinking up her story.

I made sure I could get back in, carefully closed our iron gate and tiptoed away. When I had left the house far enough behind me, I began to run, past the Town Hall and down the High Street towards the Old Bridge. The gusts seemed lighter but there was still plenty of rain and by the time I was passing Henry Williams's garage it was running from my face down my neck. Yet for all my disinclination to help Robert Ewan I was happy and excited. My mind's eye saw, not the wet and draggled Evie, her face reduced to three plums in a patch of

15

white, but Evie in her summery dress, pacing along on legs which—though some might think they were too short for perfect beauty—nevertheless reached the ground, and would do. Would do for what? The answer seemed obvious in Evie's case. She was our local phenomenon, and every male for miles round was aware of her. Perhaps it was not the breathlessness of perpetual sex that kept her lips always apart and everted, but her nose, so inadequate for breathing through, yet so perfect for pertness. Her hair would toss cloudily in a dark, shoulder length bob, as she paced, thighs motionless, legs only moving beneath the knee, her body trim and female in its walking-out uniform—a cotton frock, white socks and sandals. I had never had the luck to inspect her closely in daylight, but my furtive glances, as she passed had acquainted me with her eyelashes, too. Pounding through the darkness and rain towards the Old Bridge, I found myself thinking of paint brushes—not the delicately smoothed instrument of the artist, but the childhood one, scrubbed so hard in the dish of colour that the matted hairs are spiky and stick out all round. As I thought of those furtively glimpsed eyelashes—no, those *handfuls* of small paint brushes that flickered so delectably round Evie's eyes—I pounded harder. I never noticed the rise to the crest of the Old Bridge. Evie had none of Imogen's sacred beauty. She was strictly secular.

Nevertheless, the steep hill up to the woods brought me to a walk, and my senses. After all there was Bobby Ewan with his motor bike and his famous school and conscious superiority. There was Sergeant Babbacombe, too. When I thought of the sergeant, I stopped dead. If he knew that I had kissed—been kissed by, at anyrate—his daughter after midnight, he was likely to break my neck. Worse, speak to my parents. The courses were comparable. Sergeant Babbacombe, caretaker of the Town Hall, Keeper of the Pound, Beadle, Town Crier and any number of other offices left him by our derelict history;

16

Sergeant Babbacombe might be a figure of fun in his eighteenth-century uniform as Town Crier; thinking of him as her father, I saw rather his huge chest, meaty fists and plethoric face with its eyes so belligerently popping. I winced as I inspected for the first time an age-old question. How do such fathers have such daughters?

Then—as if she were present—I caught in my nostrils that sudden whiff of scent, and the Sergeant diminished to nothing. I hurried on up the hill, my wet trouser legs stuck to my shins, my hair dripping into my eyes. Still, there was less rain and less wind; and before I plunged into the tunnel of trees I saw a bright patch above them where the moon was trying to break through. Behind me in the valley, the church clock struck one.

There was a little more light as I neared the open area by the Leg-O'-Mutton pond. I could make out the shape of a two-seater near the edge furthest from the road, but surrounded by water. Robert Ewan moved out of the darkness under a tree and stood in the road, waiting for me.

"Young Olly?"

As I came close, I saw and heard that he was shivering more woefully than Evie; but he was making a determined attempt to ignore it. He was slight and bony, three inches taller than me, with a thatch of sandy hair and the Duke of Wellington's profile. He was clutching a mackintosh to him; and a pair of white, naked knees showed below it. Below the knees again and all down his shins were black marks, and below the marks, crumpled socks. He only had one shoe on.

"Yes it's me. Christ. You've been and gone and done it haven't you?"

"What kept you so long for God's sake? Well now you *are* here, let's get moving."

"Where's your shoe? And your trousers?"

"Sunk, laddie," said Robert, attempting nonchalance but having it interrupted by a sudden clatter of teeth. "Sunk without trace."

"I know that car! It's Bounce's car! Miss Dawlish's car!"

Robert turned the duke's profile towards it.

"Never mind that. Let's decide what to do."

"But *why*—?"

Robert took a step forward and lowered his face towards me.

"It's none of your business. But if you want to know, I was giving our young friend Babbacombe a lift over to the hop at Bumstead. I couldn't take her on the bike in this weather could I? So I borrowed Bounce's car for an hour or two. She wouldn't mind would she? Only there's no need for you to tell her."

I understood that the son of Dr. Ewan couldn't take the daughter of Sergeant Babbacombe to a dance in his father's car. Didn't have to think. Understood as by nature.

"I see."

"Satisfied?"

He stood in the road, dancing and shivering, while I took off my shoes and socks. The water was very cold, but shallow. Robert, being Robert, had not realized that there are two ways out of a pond and he had spent his time trying to shove the car backwards up hill when with half the energy he could have pushed it straight through. We got it out on the road, and while I sat on the running board and put on my socks and shoes, Robert fiddled with the plugs and wrestled with the starting handle.

By the time I was tying my shoelaces he had given up, and stood, his profile between me and the moon.

"It's no good, young Oliver. You'll have to push."

"Who? Me? Why don't you push the damn thing yourself?"

"Be reasonable, laddie. Someone's got to steer. You don't drive, do you? Besides, you're heavier than I am."

"Well—strike me pink!"

It was true all the same. Robert might be three inches taller than I was, and act always as if the three inches were twelve, but he was only half as wide. Suddenly I was shaking with rage.

"Well—Christ! You can talk! Driving the bloody car slap into the bloody pond!"

I got up and savaged my hair.

"Temper," said Robert. "If you want to know, I wasn't driving it."

"Then how the hell—"

"Do you want to stay here all night? However—we were pulled off the road under that tree up there for a spot of slap and tickle. Which reminds me—Half a mo'."

He ran off round the pond and up to the tree at the top of a slight rise, came back with his arms full.

"Floorboards."

"What the Devil?"

He opened the door of the two seater and started putting the boards back in. While he did this he spoke sometimes over his shoulder, as to a company of troops that was being jollied into an arduous but not dangerous operation.

"Not much room in these machines. Our young friend was sitting in the front seat and I took the boards out so that I could stand on the ground. Got it? Only we ran away—the old bus did. I must have sort of jerked the handbrake off with me arse, somehow. Now then, young Olly, heave O!"

It was possible, I found, by turning my back on the car, leaning against it and then thrusting with both legs, to move it up the road. Once it was moving I turned round and shoved at an angle of forty-five degrees to the horizontal. This was not too difficult. But then, without warning the car stopped dead, so that I fell spreadeagled on the rumble seat.

"Oh my guts!"

"Footbrake's a bit fierce," said Robert. "Hold on a moment, Olly. I'm dam' chilly. There's no denying it. Now we're stopped I'll just see if the old girl keeps a rug in the back, there."

"You keep driving! If this thing stops again, I'm walking home!"

I could see his profile round the side of the car and he was getting out.

"I'm perishing."

"Well, perish!"

It was mutiny. Silently Robert got back in, his teeth clattering, his shoulders, even his hands shaking. We moved off again.

I muttered.

"Bloody car. Bloody fool. Bloody footbrake—why the hell didn't you put the brake on up by the tree?"

Robert had reached his own limit. He gave a kind of whinny of rage.

"Have you ever tried running backwards down a slope with your trousers round your ankles?"

"Bloody girl, then. Why didn't *she* put on the brake?"

"How could she, with her feet up on the windscreen?"

I saw that. I pushed, grunting now and then.

"Keep moving, Olly! That's better. We're nearly at the rise. Still—she's a really sporty girl, that young Babbacombe, I give her that."

"Why?"

"She tried to steer."

Suddenly the weight of the car decreased. It stopped, as I heard Robert pull on the handbrake.

"What the—"

"We're there. Get in."

20

We were at the top of the hill where the road led out of the woods down into Stilbourne. I could make out the church tower, the huddle of houses and dark shapes of trees. I climbed in beside Robert, and settled myself. I muttered, he shivered.

"God knows how I'll push her up the High Street!"

"You're not going to have to," said Robert, the duke's profile lifted against the sky, "because there might be a copper about. Here we go!"

One hundred and twenty seconds later I had to admit that either Robert's school, or his family, or possibly even *Chums* and *The Boy's Own Paper* had given him some standards that I found not wholly contemptible. With no lights, and no engine, we leapt off the top of the Old Bridge like ski-jumpers. We shot up the High Street and across the concrete apron of Williams's garage, turned right between two sheds, then left to the open space where Robert had found the car the evening before, all under the impetus of gravity. Even then we stopped with a jerk that flattened my face against Bounce's windscreen. When I got my breath back I felt an unwilling respect for him; but we were too angry with each other for anything but the stiffest and most glacial farewell. Without speaking, we tiptoed resentfully round the Square. Robert stopped outside our gate, turned to me, and whispered coldly down from an extra twelve inches.

"Well. Thank you for your help."

I whispered back.

"Not at all. Don't mention it."

We parted, and set ourselves to our individual problems of noiseless entry. The church clock struck three.

The sun woke me, as it crawled on to my face; and instantly I remembered everything—the car, Robert, the three plums, one of them lifted, a whiff of scent. I knew, with youth's intuitive optimism, that something was not ended. Something had begun.

And there was more. The window of our bathroom not only looked out over our garden, but the Ewans's garden too. It was possible, even probable, that I should see Robert keeping fit there, and be able to crow over him. Grinning, I hurried to the bathroom. Sure enough, as soon as I looked out of the window, I saw him trot down the path, in shorts and singlet, beating the air fiercely with the padded gloves. He went trotting to the punchball rigged in the stables and struck it smartly.

"Haa!"

He danced away from it, then round it, then in again.

"Haa!"

The punchball made no reply, only quivered a bit each time he hit it. He danced away, dared it to come after him, then trotted off down the path with the handsome movements of the trained athlete, knees up, gloves up, chin down. As he turned to come back I saw that his shins were heavily armoured with white sticking plaster. He went back to the punchball. I opened the bathroom window, lathering myself vigorously, and began to laugh. Robert faltered, then attacked the punchball with fierce in-fighting.

"Any more for the Skylark?"

This time Robert did not falter. He ducked and wove. As I scraped away with my new razor, I sang raucously.

"We joined the *nay-vee* to see the world—"

Robert stopped boxing. I stared cheerfully at the brow of the hill to the north of Stilbourne, the rabbit warren spilt down the slope, the clump of trees at the top, and continued to sing.

"—we saw the pond!"

Below the immediate line of my vision, I could see that Robert was giving me a Look. It was the sort of Look that kept the Empire together, or quelled it at least. Armed with that Look and perhaps a riding crop, white men could keep order easily among the clubs and spears. He walked with great dignity into the house, duke's profile high, attention straight ahead. I laughed loud and long and savagely.

My mother expostulated fondly at breakfast.

"Oliver dear, I know you've passed all your examinations and you're going to Oxford, and heaven knows I'm glad for you to be happy—but you were making a dreadful noise in the bathroom! Whatever will the neighbours think?"

I answered her indistinctly.

"Young Ewan. Laughing at him."

"*Not* with your mouth full, dear!"

"Sorry."

"Bobby Ewan. It's such a pity that you—Still he's been away at school most of the time." This telegraphic style was entirely comprehensible to me. It meant that my mother was regretting the social difference between the Ewans and ourselves. She was thinking too of the incompatibility that had magnified the difference and exacerbated it. As small children, socially innocent, so to speak, we had played together; and I knew things about that play which had reached neither Mrs. Ewan nor my mother. We had hardly been out of our respective prams.

"You're my slave."

"No I'm not."

"Yes you are. My father's a doctor and yours is only his dispenser."

That was why I pushed him off the wall into the Ewans's cucumber frame, where he made a very satisfactory crash. Not surprisingly we drifted apart after that, and what with school and motor bikes and careful parents, the most we ever did was to snipe at each other with our air guns, aiming always to miss. Now I had kissed Evie Babbacombe—well,

23

more or less—and had seen Robert make a fool of himself.

"Oliver, dear—I do wish you wouldn't whistle with your mouth full!"

After breakfast I went as casually as I could to the dispensary, where my father was making pills, in the old-fashioned way. I stood in the doorway that led from our cottage into the dispensary thinking consciously for the first time how much more like a doctor he looked than staid Dr. Ewan, or the junior partner, reedy Dr. Jones. Such a visit was not usual, and my father looked round ponderously under his heavy brows but said nothing. I leaned against the wall by the door and wondered what excuse I could find for going through into the reception room where Evie would be working. Perhaps, I thought, my father would agree that I needed a thorough overhaul; and indeed, my heart seemed to be acting up in an unusual manner. But before I had got round to saying anything, Evie—who must have been equipped with antennae like my mother—appeared at the end of the passage. She was wearing her blue and white cotton dress, and respectable stockings under her white socks; for of course she could not sit at the desk in the reception room with bare legs. She had one finger on her lips and was shaking her head severely. Her face was different. The orbital area of her left eye was swollen so that on the left side her paint brushes were motionless, their tips projecting in a rigid line. The right side made up for this inactivity; but I had little time to inspect her in detail since she so clearly had a message for me. The finger on the lips, the shaken head—that, I could understand. Don't say anything to anybody about anything! Sensible enough and not really necessary; but those weaving motions with both hands at her throat as if she were trying to avoid strangulation, that hand then so fiercely stabbing with the fore-finger in the general direction of the Square —and now the head, nodding this time, the bob flying—.

24

Evie stopped moving. Listened. Disappeared into the reception room, the door closing without a sound. My father was still making pills. Casually, I lounged back into the cottage and sat myself at the piano. I played, thinking. It was always a useful cover. What did she want with the Square? And who was going to strangle her? Sergeant Babbacombe was the obvious candidate but was hardly likely to do it in the doctor's reception room. Perhaps she wanted me to go out into the Square so that she could pass me a message—say, in the High Street? It would be hours before she could get away from her desk. But she could make some excuse or other. What was more and more delightfully evident was that Evie Babbacombe wanted to meet me. Not Robert. Me!

I strolled into the Square, and stood, hands in pockets, inspecting the sky. It was bright blue, in a cooperative sort of way. I waited, hoping she would appear and that I could follow her to whatever private place was suitable for such a meeting, but the minutes lengthened, then dragged, and still she did not come. What came at last, was Sergeant Babba-combe. He marched out from under the pillars of the Town Hall and stood at attention, facing the length of the Square to the church. He was carrying his brass handbell and wearing his Town Crier's dress—buckled shoes, white cotton stockings, red knee breeches, red waistcoat, cotton ruffle, blue frock coat, and blue, three-cornered hat. He rang the handbell, staring belligerently over his chest at the church tower. Then he bawled.

"Ho yay, ho yay, ho yay! Lost. In Chandler's Lane, between the chaplofese and Chandler's Close. Hay gold cross hand chain. With the hinitials hee bee. Hand the hinscription 'Hamor vinshit Homniar.' Ther finder will be rewarded."

He rang the bell again, lifted his three-cornered hat towards the sky and uttered the loyal shout.

"God hsave-ther KING!"

He put his hat on, turned right, and marched off with steps of regulation thirty inches towards the corner of Mill Lane to do it all over again. Hee bee! Evie Babbacome! I saw it all. The cross was to be found and returned to her in strictest secrecy. Not a word about woods or ponds. Probably not a word about a hop at Bumstead. I knew exactly what I was to do.

With that capacity for long and deep calculation which has since proved so beneficial to my country I set myself to evaluate the situation. Evie wanted her gold cross. I wanted Evie. A return to that place where she had proved so accessible to Robert might solve the problem for us both. Panic-stricken and furtive, she would steal off to look herself, given the chance; and my most delicate calculation was involved with getting us both there at the same time. I knew the working arrangements of the Ewans's practice as well as I knew anything. I knew the times that Evie could pretend she had stayed behind to clear up, or sort the files. She might even invent an emergency as cover for her own. Because if some stroller in the woods saw the cross glittering among the twigs and empty acorn cups and turned it in to Sergeant Babbacombe, Evie was due for the shiner to outshine all shiners. She might even qualify, if rumour was not entirely a lying jade, for the sergeant's army belt with its buckle and rows of shining brass studs. When I thought of the rumoured belt and the chance I had of preserving her from it, I felt a twinge of noble sympathy amid my tenseness and excitement.

I went through the cottage and got my bike. I rode down the High Street and very carefully over the Old Bridge, since Sergeant Babbacombe was reciting his piece again on the crest of it. I pushed my bike up the hill, then freewheeled down to the pond.

Everything was different, and the same. The water was still. The woods were still, yet they hummed and buzzed under the sun. There was green dapple, flash of a dragonfly over the water, whirl and dance of flies. I pushed my bike up the rise from the pond and leaned it against the gigantic oak bole. I looked round, then carefully followed the shallow tracks down to the pond. I found no gold cross, but only a muddy shoe. I threw the shoe towards some clear grass in front of a flowering bush and stood, staring down at the brown water. There was nothing for it. This would have to be a proper scientific search, like quartering the desert for a crashed plane. The cross might be—probably was—in the pond. But the sensible thing to do was to look in the easy places first.

I went back to the oak and inspected every inch of ground near the tracks. When I had cleared an area, I laid broken twigs at each corner; and presently I had a pattern of them all the way from the oak to the edge of the pond. But I could not find the cross. There was nothing for it. I took off my socks and shoes and stepped into the water. Every time I moved I stirred up mud and had to wait for it to settle again; and even then, I could not pretend that I could see the bottom at all clearly. In the end, I was reduced to groping blindly with my fingers. Every now and then, I stuck twigs upright so that their ends showed. All I found, was a pair of twisted-up trousers, deeply embedded.

I paddled back and sat moodily under the oak tree, waiting for my feet to dry. I went over my calculations again, but this time I was interrupted. A sound as of a rocket, climbed the hill from Stilbourne and roared down the road through the woods. When the motor bike reached the pond, I heard it slow, then come revving and backfiring across the grass to the other side of the oak tree. It coughed to a stop.

"Hop off, m'dear!"

Evie, like a good soldier's daughter, had mobilized all her forces.

27

"Well, well," said Robert. "Well, well, well! Whom have we here? *But* whom have we here?"

Evie came running round the tree after him.

"Have you found it, Olly?"

"No. Sorry."

Evie clasped her hands. Wrung them.

"Oh dear, oh dear!"

She didn't seem to be wearing anything but the cotton frock, unless you count the socks and sandals. Perhaps she hadn't wanted to risk her stockings on the back of the motor bike. Perhaps she just didn't like wearing them. When I tore my eyes away from the rest of her, I saw that now the swelling round her left eye had spread down into the cheek. Her other bright, grey eye was very wide open among the motionless paintbrushes—wide open and anxious.

"How's your face feeling, Evie?"

"It's all right now. Doesn't hurt a bit. I hit it on the door you know. It hurt dreadfully then. Oh look—we *must* find that cross! Suppose somebody's found it already! Dad'll 'alf-well—"

Robert laid a hand on her shoulder. He spoke kindly but firmly.

"Now don't get in a tizzy, young Babbacombe. It's just a question of looking."

"I've looked."

"We'll look again."

"What d'you think all those twigs are? I conducted a scientific search. The only thing left is to drain the pond. By the way, your trousers are hanging on that bush to dry."

"Thanks," said Robert stiffly. He looked towards the bush. "My God, young Olly! You might have got some of the mud off!"

"Well damn me!"

"Olly! Bobby! Boys!"

"I'd have found it for you if I could."

"Somebody's probably pinched it", said Robert. "Ha! The scientific search—inch by inch and still couldn't find it. Well, we've only got your word for that, young Oliver!"

"Just exactly what do you mean to imply?"

"Scientific stuff," said Robert, still laughing down his profile. "Great brain and all that stuff—"

A brilliant insult occurred to me.

"I turned his pockets out, Evie, but it wasn't there. He probably put it in his breast pocket. Ask him, will you?"

"Olly! Bobby! I got to be back at surg'ry in half an hour!"

Robert had stopped laughing. He had gone very still, very calm. He patted her shoulder.

"Now don't you worry, m'dear."

I laughed jeeringly.

"Did you feel a sharp tug at your neck last night?"

"No. 'Course not. What a thing!"

One side of her face giggled, then was solemn again. Robert paced slowly to the bush and hung his jacket by the trousers. He took off the silk square from under his open shirt and stuffed it in the jacket. He came back just as slowly.

"If you'd care to stroll round the other side of the tree, young Babbacombe—"

"Why? What you going to do?"

"I'm going to give this young oaf the lesson he obviously needs."

He turned to me, a good fifteen inches higher up in the air, and jerked his head sideways.

"Come on you. This way."

He stalked off round the bush. I glanced at Evie questioningly. She was staring after him, hands clasped up by her neck, lips wide apart. I picked my way after him with my naked feet among the twigs and acorn cups. On the other side of the bush was a glade, an open length of perfect turf between walls of high green bracken. Robert was waiting for me, and pulled aside a thorny sucker with awesome courtesy so that I could step through. Then he faced me from a few yards away, his jaw set, limbs loose. He reminded me vaguely of something—an illustration in a book perhaps. He addressed me as if he too were remembering a book.

"Which way would you care to face?"

We fought of course at my Grammar School after our fashion. We couldn't afford boxing gloves and punch balls and that sort of thing. Besides, I was Head Boy, and a dedicated chemist. I had put such childish pastimes behind me.

"I don't box."

"This will teach you. Are you going to apologize?"

"I'll see you in hell first."

Robert turned his left shoulder towards me, put up his fists, lowered his chin into them and came dancing in. I put my own fists up, left fist forward, though I was what Robert would have called in his knowledgeable way a "South paw". My left hand octave-technique always had an effortless brilliance which was very impressive until you detected the fumbling inadequacy of my right hand. But Robert was not a piano. I saw his left arm shoot out its bony length, and half the woods exploded into an electric white star. I made a dab at him in return; but he was already three yards away, flicking his sandy head, his feet dancing, as he prepared to come in again. I made another dab through the red circles that were now expanding and contracting in front of my right eye, but Robert was somewhere else. His right arm came round and my left ear—indeed, all the woods—rang with a mellow and continuous note. Apart from my hands, I have always been a bit clumsy, a bit ungainly; and now, with Robert dancing so unattainably beyond my north paw or whatever the technical term was, I began to move from irritation, through anger, to rage. The blows themselves—and my right eye produced another electric star—were no more than an irritant, flick, flick, tap! It was his invulnerability that was making me pant and sweat. I abandoned all attempt to imitate him; so feeling him near me beyond the red rings, I hit him with my octave technique, fortissimo, sforzando, in the pit of the stomach. It was lovely. His breath and his spit came out in my face. He hung himself over me, his long arms beating feebly at my sides as he reached for his breath without finding it. One shoe scraped excruciatingly down my naked instep. I howled and jerked it up, and my knee fitted itself neatly between his legs. Robert bent double with extraordinary swiftness, his mouth open, both fists clamped in his crutch. I swung my left fist in three-quarters of a circle so that it was still whistling upward when it smashed his nose. He went over backwards into the bracken by the side of the glade and disappeared.

The red rings were dwindling, the mellow note diminishing. I stood, bare-footed in the glade, the sweat streaming down me. My teeth were clenched so tightly that they hurt. The only noises I could hear outside the storm in my head were faint ones from Robert, hidden somewhere in the bracken. They were variations on the theme of "Ooo". The first I heard was very delicate, prolonged, and ended with an upward inflection, as if he were posing some intimate question to himself. The next was just as long, and very tender, as if he had found the answer. The third was utter abandonment. My own chest was going in and out, and I had a sudden urge to run and put my shoes on, then come back and jump up and down on him.

"Olly! Bobby! Where are you?"

It was Evie, threshing about somewhere in the bracken. Still with my fists and teeth clenched I shouted as loudly as I could.

31

"Here! Where d'you think?"

She appeared for a moment.

"Where is he? What have you done to him? Bobby!"

She disappeared again. Robert's head and shoulders rose out of the bracken. One hand held a scarlet and sopping handkerchief to his face. The other was out of sight—probably still between his legs. Even then, he essayed a sort of nonchalant courtesy through the bloody linen.

"Frifling infury. Hofpital. Outfashients. 'Fscuse—"

He waded away. Evie was still hidden.

"Bobb—*ee*—Where are you?"

She broke out into the glade, came tripping along it, socks and sandals flicking this way and that. On the other side of the bracken the motor bike started and rattled away in a decrescendo. Evie stopped.

"There! How am I going to get home? It's all your fault! And he's going off to Cranwell tomorrow! It was the last—"

"Last what?"

She turned back to me. Her one eye was very bright, and she was breathing as quickly as I was. She gave a scandalized laugh.

"Boys are awful!"

"Spoilt his beauty for him at any rate."

"Your shirt's wringing wet—look. It's sticking to you."

"Cadet Officer Ewan, the Noseless Wonder. That's what he'll be."

I caught another whiff of her, through the rank smell of my own sweat. I grabbed her by the wrist and pulled her close. My teeth had unclenched themselves but my heart had started to pound all over again.

"Evie—"

The woods swam.

"I'll—I'll drain the pond for you."

Her paintbrushes shivered. Inside them, one eyeball rolled up. Her lips curled farther open as I bent towards them.

32

"Listen! There!"

I tried to draw her close; but she was stronger than Robert and shoved me away. She moved in a panic. From the valley, I could hear the church clock striking.

"Third time I been late this week!"

She plunged into the bracken and I plunged after her but my naked feet found a mass of thistles so that I danced and howled.

"Wait for me, Evie!"

"It's surg'ry already!"

I pulled the more obvious of the prickles out, then crawled through, back the way Robert and I had come. His trousers and jacket still hung on the bush, and there was a shoe under it. I rolled down my own trouser legs and got my own shoes and socks on as quickly as I could. Evie was fifty yards up the road by the time I was ready to go after her. She would walk, then run for a bit with her bob flopping, then walk again. The most I thought I could salvage out of this encounter was an arrangement for another meeting, so I rode fast and skidded to a spectacular stop ahead of her.

"There's a good idea! Don't look round—"

She was hitching her skirt up nearly to her waist. She was wearing short white knickers under them with white embroidery round the edges. She sat astride the carrier of my bike and the carrier groaned.

"You *are* a pet! Hurry!"

By putting my full weight on one pedal, I could just about get the bike moving. We wobbled off up the road.

"I shall be ever so late."

I exerted what strength I had left and started to sweat again. We worked up a fair speed.

"Oliver—I believe he left his jacket behind, as well as—I don't know what Mrs. Ewan's going to say! After we've got back, you wouldn't like to—"

"To what?"

"Somebody ought to fetch them for him."

I gave a kind of snarl, put up one hand to wipe the hair and sweat out of my eyes and nearly fell off.

"Careful!"

There was a sudden flood of light, so though my eyes watched the road under my front wheel I knew we were out of the woods and at the top of the hill. I sat back, allowing gravity to do the rest. The church clock stood at a quarter past the hour.

"Aren't you going a bit fast?"

I put both brakes on. They dragged for a moment, then our speed increased again. I gripped them hard but they had no effect. I heard a shriek from behind me and then the rise of the Old Bridge approached us at about sixty miles an hour. As we struck it there came a grinding clatter from the carrier, a loud bang from my rear tire and a wail from Evie. The bike seemed to stop in its own length; and her weight nearly sent me over the handlebars. She detached herself from the carrier and stood for a moment, beating her bottom with both hands.

"Tore my dress I think—no. It's all right."

"Hang on a minute!"

"I *got* to go."

"Can't we—"

"P'raps. I don't know. Thanks anyway for the lift."

She scurried over the bridge and vanished down the other side. I examined my bike. The carrier and the rear mudguard had wrapped themselves round the wheel. The tyre was flat. I cursed and struggled with the wreckage. At last I managed to disentangle it, jerking the mudguard away from the tattered rubber. I pushed my bike bumpety-bump over the bridge. Evie was progressing up the High Street in the same way as she had come from the pond—a little run, then a walk, then a little run again. Suddenly she quickened her pace and kept it up; but she was too late. Tiny, birdlike Mrs. Babba-combe with her grey cloche hat and shopping basket had seen her. She ran across the road, grabbed Evie by the elbow and kept hold of it. They went up the street side by side, Mrs. Babbacombe making pecks and nags at her daughter's shoulder. I thought with ungenerous satisfaction that Evie would have to think fast, to get out from under that one. I went bumping up the street and then turned in over the concrete apron of the garage to find Henry; but when I saw where he was I went on wheeling my bike in a semicircle to come out again. He was standing in white overalls, his hands on his hips, looking at Miss Dawlish's little two-seater.

"Master Oliver—"

"Oh hullo Henry. I thought you were busy. I wasn't going to bother you."

Henry bent down and examined my back wheel. I looked over *him* at the two-seater and my feet froze to the concrete. It might have been sunk for a year or two in a swamp.

"*Dyma vi,*" said Henry. "That's a bad split, indeed it is. You've been giving some other lad a lift, haven't you? Well now. We shan't get any more use out of that!"

I heard a soft hissing behind me. Captain Wilmot pulled up beside us in his electric invalid carriage.

"Hullo Henry. Is my other battery ready?"

"Not for another hour, Captain," said Henry. "Just take a look at this!"

He went over to the two-seater.

"Hold on," said Captain Wilmot. "I'll stretch me legs for a bit. Don't go, young Oliver. I want to hear about the team."

He began to manoeuvre in the basketwork chair, grunting and gritting his teeth.

"Fix bayonets!"

Captain Wilmot was a war wreck, adequately pensioned, provided with transport, and a secretarial job at the hospital

35

for which he was, as he said, remunerated with an honorarium. The shell that had buried him had also filled him full of metal fragments in unexcavatable places. The rude wits of Chandler's Close, where he lived in the cottage opposite Sergeant Babbacombe, always said that he rattled far more than his chair. He was deaf in one ear from the shell. Cotton wool hung out of it. He secreted, heavily.

"I've got to get away. I—"

"For God's sake! Stay where you are."

He was testy. This was because he was getting out of his carriage. Whenever he was getting in or out of his carriage he was testy. Indeed, if you caught a glimpse of his face before he had rearranged it you could sometimes see a sort of animal savagery there as if the force that lifted him had been sheer hate. Yet he was fond of young people and of youth generally —perhaps because his own had been blown out of him before he had had any use from it; a junior clerk whose country needed him. He gave his services free to the team on the miniature rifle range at our grammar school. After endless manoeuvring he would sit by us as we lay at the firing point, giving advice and encouragement.

"Don't pull, boy! Your foresight's going up and down like a bucket in a well! *Squeeze*—like this."

Then you would feel a handful of your gluteus maximus massaged and squeezed for a few moments.

"Now what do you think of that, Captain?"

Captain Wilmot inched forward on his two sticks and examined the car closely.

"Been through a barrage by the looks of it."

My feet were not frozen to the concrete. They were buried in it.

"Joy Riding they call it," said Henry. "Young blackguards. I'd give them joy riding." He opened the door and poked about inside. "Here. Look at this!"

36

He backed out and turned round. In his hand he held a gold cross and chain.

"Well now, a cross is a thing Miss Dawlish never wore in her life, I'm certain!"

Captain Wilmot leaned over Henry's hand.

"Are you sure, Henry? I've seen it somewhere—"

Henry brought it close to his eyes.

" 'I.H.S.' There's writing on the other side too. 'E.B. Amor vincit omnia.' What would that mean, then?"

Captain Wilmot turned to me.

"Come on, young Oliver. You're the scholar of the party."

I was cold inside from fear, and hot outside from embarrassment.

"I think it means, 'Love beats everything'."

"E.B.," said Henry. "Evie Babbacombe!"

He lifted his sad, brown eyes to my face and kept them there.

"I knew I'd seen it before," said Captain Wilmot. "Lives next door. Comes to me for lessons y'know. Correspondence and filin' and all that. She wears it under her dress, down between here."

"She used to work here," said Henry, his eyes still on my face, "before she went to the doctor's. I expect that's when it got lost."

"Of course," said Captain Wilmot, "she doesn't always wear it down under her dress. If she's not wearin' her beads, she wears it outside, down between here. Well, I must get on."

He turned laboriously back to his carriage, saying no more about the battery or the team. He grinned at us, a grin that went savage as he lowered himself. He stowed his two sticks, turned the carriage in its own length and hissed away.

Henry continued to look at me. A blush started rising irresistibly from the soles of my feet. It surged to my shoulders, shot down my arms, so that my hands bloated on

37

the handle bars. It filled my face, my head—till even my hair seemed burning with it.

"Well now," said Henry at last. "Evie Babbacombe."

The two oil-smeared lads who had been taking apart the engine of a lorry were standing and looking at us with grins only less savage than the Captain's. As if he had four eyes instead of two, Henry wheeled on them.

"Do you lads think I pay you to stand about all day with your mouths open? I want those valves ready by half-past five!"

I muttered.

"Give it to her if you like. I'll give it to her—"

Henry turned back to me. I unstuck one hand and held it out. He swung the cross above it by the chain like a pendulum, looked closely at me.

"You don't drive yet, do you, Master Oliver?"

"No. No. I don't drive."

Henry nodded and dropped the cross in my palm.

"With the compliments of the management."

He turned back and burrowed into the car. I wheeled my bumpety bike away, the cross clenched in one hand, my feet able to move at last. I had only one thought in my head as I went towards our cottage.

That was a near thing.

After I had put my bike away I went through into the dispensary, where my father was squinting down a microscope under the window.

"Henry," I said, swinging the cross casually. "Henry Williams. Miss Babbacombe left this thing down there when she was working in his garage." I threw it up and caught it effortlessly. "Asked me to give it to her," I said. "I expect she'll be in the reception room won't she? I'll just go through—"

I walked down the short passage and opened the door. Evie was sitting behind the desk and trying to inspect her left eye with her right one in a small round mirror. She saw me in it, instead.

"Olly! You musn't come—"

"Here you are. Thought you'd like this."

With an attempt at Robert's nonchalance I tossed the cross on the desk. Evie pounced on it with a delighted cry.

"My cross!"

She put down the mirror and busied herself, fixing the chain round her neck. Her face went solemn and she bent her head. She muttered, made some quick movements over her breasts with one hand. In our local complex of State Church, Nonconformity, and massive indifference, I had never seen anything like them. She looked up at me and smiled suddenly with open mouth, one eye blinking. She whispered with a kind of gleeful accusation.

"Olly! You story!"

"What d'you mean?"

She pushed back her chair an inch or two, then sat, looking up, her hands grasping the edge of the desk. She examined me as if she had never seen me before.

"Evie—when can we—"

"That'd be telling, wouldn't it?"

There was no doubt at all. Evie Babbacombe, ripest apple on the tree, was regarding me with approval and positive admiration!

There came a voice, resounding from the depths of the doctor's house.

"Miss Babbacombe!"

She jumped up, patting back her bob, and went to the door into the surgery. She stopped by it and looked back. Giggled.

"You had it all the time!"

39

I took my outrage with me back into the dispensary. My father was still at the microscope, adjusting the slide with minute movements of his big fingers. I left well alone and went through into the cottage, wondering what to do. If Sergeant Babbacombe got her story out of her, by third degree or other means, he might not admire my imagined part in it as much as she did. This was an emergency. I had to see her before she went home; but I could think of no excuse for going back through the dispensary. On the other hand, if I stood sideways by my bedroom window I could see down into the Square and the steps of the Ewans's house next door. As soon as she appeared, I could go down stairs again and through into our garden. If my mother was in the kitchen or scullery I could account for these movements easily enough. ("Just going to have a look at my bike.") In the garden, I could accelerate, nip over the garden wall into Chandler's Lane, pound along past the bottom of the Ewans's garden, the vicarage garden and the three cottages where the lane turned down towards Chandler's Close, then come back between the vicarage and the churchyard. By this means I should be entering the Square from the opposite direction and could meet her accidentally. I went to my station therefore, and stood close to the chintz curtains. It was long wait, but I could take no chances. Then, just when I was expecting her at any moment, I heard a heavy and martial tread approaching under my window from the other direction. Sergeant Babbacombe was coming from the Town Hall. He was not taking his usual route, past Wertwhistle Wertwhistle and Wertwhistle, Solicitors, Miss Dawlish's bow window and the rest. He was coming along this side on a course which would lead him straight to our front gate. It was not my actions during the past twenty four hours that put me in an instant panic. It was my intentions. For under the forward angle of his three-cornered hat, his face wore such a plethoric

40

and parental animosity it took my breath away. His meaty fists swung low as he marched along, the metal studs of his shoes struck sparks from the cobbles. Then—as if she had been watching from a window too—Evie came tripping down the steps from the Ewans's door. She was wearing a head square of white silk tied under her chin and the free corners flipped as she moved. She wore stockings of course. She was laughing and smiling, hands up by her shoulders, calves moving outward, bottom rotating a little. She tripped up to Sergeant Babbacombe, close, laughing up in his face, almost vertically up.

"Look, Dad! I'd left it in the Ladies' Toilet at the surg'ry all the time! Silly me!"

He marched straight on. She got out of his way and turned to go with him. He was going far faster than she could, with his long strides, so every now and then she had to trip again, with a burst of gay laughter. Once in position, she felt for his hand, leaning sideways towards him, head on one side, her body stretching so that her silk square crept up towards his shoulder. He would get a stride ahead and she would trip again, still feeling for his hand. She got it at last. It stopped swinging. Without slackening his march, the Sergeant's fingers shifted from her palm to her wrist. After that she no longer tripped, but kept up with him in a constant running movement of quick little steps. She had to.

I went downstairs, into the garden, and began to pace round our little lawn with my hands in my trouser pockets. Between my lust for Evie's trim femininity and my fear of her bloodshot father were a whole host of other less immediately pressing considerations. Henry might drop a word somewhere; though I had a simple and unconscious faith in Henry. Captain Wilmot might drop one. Robert—and now that my rage was gone I was worried about him—Robert might be badly hurt. My own left ear felt warm still and my

41

right eye, while not as bad as Evie's, was nevertheless tender. It watered easily. Also there was Imogen. I came to a halt on the grass and stared at a belated bee which was fumbling over a spike of delphinium. I realized in a puzzled kind of way that I had not thought of Imogen for hours and hours. She came back into my mind and pushed my heart down as usual; but this time in a way that I was quite unable to understand. She made my pursuit of Evie not only urgent and inevitable; the mere thought of her quickened me to desperation. It was—and even then I felt the absurdity of it—as if since she had got engaged to be married I was forced into some sort of competition with her and him. I began to pace round and round again. I felt like a fly in treacle.

The next morning, when I was shaving, I saw Robert trot into the garden for a final pre-Cranwell bout with his punchball. The sight made me embarrassed. Our fight had been a typical one between his sort of boy and my sort, as described in all juvenile literature. He was clear cut, clean-limbed. He had a straight left. I was strong, square, and clumsy; an oaf, in fact. Despite this, I had won. Moreover, I had won in the way an oaf might be expected to—the only way indeed, permitted to him—by cheating. I had stuck my knee in his balls. It was useless to tell myself it had been an accident; for I knew that after he was doubled over, helpless, I had felt an instant of black malice, cruel joy, and sheer *intention* before I hit him with my fist. It was a bit more treacle. There he was, down there, dancing with his athlete's limber movements round the motionless ball; and I could see that he had sticking plaster on his nose now, as well as his shins. Here was I, devious and calculating, with a different accent, and unable to drive a car. When I saw that he had finished his workout and was about to trot back to the house, I stuck my halfscraped face out of the window and waved my safety razor at him.

"Wotcher Robert! Going off today? Good luck!"

Robert cut me dead. He hoisted the duke of Wellington's profile into the air with all its plaster and carried it straight through into the house. I did not laugh. I was humiliated and ashamed.

Nor was it easy, however I contrived and loitered, to meet our mutual friend, young Babbacombe. She was on the hook. She was padlocked and bolted, chained. Each day, Sergeant Babbacombe brought her to work, stood watching her through the door, then went on to set out the chairs in the Town Hall; or gather them and stack them up; or collect the pennies from the locks in the public lavatories; or hoist the union jack; or ring his brass bell at stations round the town to proclaim a whist drive at the Working Men's Institute or a fete in the vicarage garden. Mrs. Babbacombe usually fetched her. At normal times Mrs. Babbacombe radiated a social awareness and friendliness that was indomitable, though seldom reciprocated. She was a sparrow of a woman, neat like Evie, but already wizened. She moved quickly, head up and turning from person to person, smiling—sometimes inclining her head, aiming it right across the High street in a gracious, sideways bow to a person entirely out of her social sphere. Naturally these greetings were never acknowledged or even mentioned; since no one could tell whether Mrs. Babbacombe was mad, and believed herself entitled to make them, or whether she came from some fabulous country where the Town Crier's wife and the wife of the Chief Constable might be on terms of intimacy. The first alternative seemed the more probable. You might see her, shall we say, chirping like a sparrow at the counter of the International Stores, then smiling graciously (head on left shoulder slight inclination of the neck) at Lady Hamilton-Smythe who was apparently unaware of her existence. She was about our only Roman Catholic, was Mrs. Babbacombe—unless you include

43

Evie—and that, taken with her other eccentricity, made her notable and trying. Since she would not mix with the riff-raff of Chandler's Close and nobody else spoke to her, it seemed strange that she persevered with her useless smiles and bows. However, for a few days after the episode of the cross, the smiles and bows were absent. Sergeant Babbacombe delivered Evie like a parcel and little Mrs. Babbacombe collected her, wizened and grim.

After a week, Evie came into the dispensary complaining of a headache and my father fixed her up with something. That evening when Mrs. Babbacombe came to the steps of the Ewans's house, the two ladies left together, laughing and chattering like old friends. It was a remarkable change, and went still further. Evie was let off the hook, having done this bit of penance. A few evenings later—it must have been about nine o'clock—Evie came pacing along by herself on the other side of the square. She wore her cotton summer dress, no stockings, white socks and sandals. She slid along, lips breathlessly everted, slight smile enchanting the evening air, bob glossy, both eyes by this time shining bright, only her legs moving below the knees. We were back to square one. And mysterious as a glowworm, she was emitting a radiance of desirability so strong as to be almost visible light. As she came near Miss Dawlish's bow window opposite our cottage, her pace slowed till it was imperceptible. Nor was it my imagination that even at that distance I could see a mad fluttering of the black paintbrushes and the flash of eyes swivelling in my direction. As if commanded by a master I stole out of the house.

Evie was sliding past the Town Hall down the High Street. There were very few people about unless you count a police-man and the girl in the box office of the cinema. With a proper sense of taboo I followed her at a distance of fifty yards. This was difficult since she did not seem to have the same social

44

awareness and moved at a snail's pace. Indeed I was forced to examine the Saddler's window, the Tobacconist's, and the less likely seductions of the Needlework Shop in order to maintain my proper distance. When she reached the Old Bridge she went no further. In the conflict between social propriety and sexual attraction there was never much doubt which would win. Besides, the sun had set, night was coming on and already the darkness had settled under the arch of the bridge. Above it, there was a degree of twilight. Evie had arranged herself, leaning with her bottom on the stone coping at the top of the rise. She was watching the place where the sun had gone down. I went up to her. We were surprised to see each other.

"How's your eye, Evie?"

"Quite, quite all right. How's yours?"

I had forgotten my own injuries. I pressed my hand into the socket of my right eye.

"Seems all right."

"You heard from Bobby?"

I was so surprised that I did not answer for a moment.

"No. Why should I?"

Evie did not reply for a while. She leaned her head back and smiled at me out of the corner of her eye.

"You've got a lot of time to spare haven't you, Olly?"

"I'm off school."

It was difficult to take my eyes off her, for not only was she exhaling her individual light, she was breathing out the scent of flowers and pretty things with embroidery on them, and girl's laughter an octave higher than a man's. Nevertheless I managed to glance sideways, and as I did so the sodium lamps shivered on all the way up the High Street towards the Square, each plucking itself out of the twilight. We were not invisible.

"Let's go for a walk."

45

"Where is there?"

"We could stroll up the hill."

"Dad wouldn't like me to go in the woods. Not after dark."

A pair of trousers deeply embedded in mud flashed through my mind, then hung themselves on a bush to dry.

"But—"

It was staggering and infuriating. She was defended, bland, secure. The dregs of the western day glinted in one eye, sodium light in the other. I took a step or two, then stood, looking back.

"Come on, Evie—we can go along by the river."

She shook her head so that the bob flew, then settled.

"Dad says I mustn't."

I knew why, without having to think. That way led through fields to Hotton where the racing stables were. Sergeant Babbacombe probably envisaged stable lads lurking lecherously behind every bush; and he may very well have been right.

"Well then—We could go the other way along the river, round Pillicock."

Evie shut her mouth, and shook her head again, smiling mysteriously.

"Why not?"

No answer; just the glint, smile and shake. Each time the bob flew it seemed to release a new cloud of scented suggestion. I thought in bewilderment of what reason she might have for this other geographical prohibition. The most notable thing in that direction was a famous boarding school, keeping itself very much to itself, though only half-a-dozen fields away from us. Perhaps Sergeant Babbacombe had ideas about that too? "Don't let me catch you playing about with the young college gents, my girl—they're devils, they are!" But for whatever reason, the countryside was closing in round us. To the south, the erotic woods, west the racing

46

stables, east, the college, and to the north, nothing but the escarpment of the bare downs—and here we were, visible, the pair of us on the crest of the Old Bridge.

As if this confinement made Evie happy, she began to hum, nodding her head in time.

"Boop-a-doop, boop-a-doop!"

The blood surged in my head. I said something, I couldn't tell what. I needed a club or a flint axe. Evie looked up at me, surprised.

"Don't you like them?"

"Who?"

"On the wireless. The Savoy Orpheans. I listen to them every night."

The surge became a rage from head to foot.

"I hate them! Hate them! Cheap—trivial—"

Then we were silent, both of us, while the rage died down in me and settled to a steady trembling. When Evie spoke at last it was very coldly and haughtily.

"Well. I'm sorry, I'm sure!"

I was getting nowhere, that was certain. But while I was wondering what to do next, Evie gleamed up at me and smiled.

"That music you were playing yesterday, Olly, I liked that. You know—on the piano."

"Chopin. Study in C minor, opus twenty five, number twelve."

"You *can* play loud!"

"Oh I don't know—"

I thought for a moment. When I was practising the semi-quaver passages of the Appassionata, or the left hand octaves of the Polonaise in A flat major, if my father had left the door into the dispensary open, he would sometimes close it gently. He was very musical himself and could not afford to be distracted at moments when his work was particularly delicate.

47

"I didn't know you passed our house, Evie!"

"I was in the reception room, silly!"

I was a little surprised at this. After all, there was the sitting room door, a passage, the door through to the dispensary, another passage and another door between the reception room and our yellowing keys. Perhaps I *could* play loud.

"It's just practice. I do it for fun."

"When I left after morning surgery you were playing it. When I came back for evening surgery there you were again! You must like music a lot, Olly. How long were you playing?"

"I do. All day."

"It's nice. You must play it for me some time. Dr. Ewan likes it too."

"Honestly?"

"He came into the reception room yesterday after Mrs. Miniver left and said was that you still playing."

"Did he say anything else?"

"Not much. Just how glad he was that you were going to Oxford."

I was deeply gratified. I had not known that Dr. Ewan was musical too. I was trying to learn the Chopin study, because those wild broken chords, that storm of notes had seemed so exactly to express and contain my own dry-mouthed and hopeless passion for Imogen Greatley; but the technical difficulties were enormous and obsessed me. I explained. "There's a note—G natural—I have to hit it in passing with this finger, you see—"

I held my right forefinger up close to her face. She took it in both hands and examined it, pulling it about.

"Ow! Careful! It's a bit sore—"

Laughing aloud, Evie pulled and pulled. Instantly the ice broke up and cascaded away. With shouts and giggles we wrestled in the sodium-lighted twilight. In some way that

48

was not clear to me I changed from pursued to pursuer and Evie was trying to escape.

"No! No, Olly! You mustn't—"

She was close to me, hard against my chest. She ceased to struggle.

"You mustn't. Someone'll see us."

I grabbed her wrist and lugged her off the rise of the bridge, down to where the pier was set, half on land, half in water. The sodium lights were out of sight. She had stopped laughing and I had started trembling again. The only light came from Evie, her three black plums so close to me against the pier, but now with no hair smeared across them, no trickling rain, and the exhalation of mysterious perfume constant and maddening. I pressed against her, my loins stirring, my body burning. I got all the kisses I wanted. I got more kisses than I wanted. I didn't get anything else.

The church clock struck. Evie changed from a girl whose strength was barely sufficient to protect her from assault unless it was reinforced by warm and pathetic pleading, to one who could carry coal and chop wood. Since my head was still whirling I was not ready for the change, and her thrust with both arms sent me backwards halfway down the bank.

"There! And Mum said—"

She was scrambling up to the road. I scrambled after her, pushing clods out of the earth. I caught up with her on the bridge.

"Evie—Let's come here tomorrow night. Or can't we go for a walk or something?"

She had resumed her movement in the sodium lights.

"I can't stop you meeting me, can I? It's a free country."

"Tomorrow then—"

"If you like."

She moved on up the High Street. As my wits settled I became aware of people, and of the delicate radii of influences

49

that we were approaching. Halfway up the street one of my masters lived—or had his rooms—over a shop. At the Town Hall, the area controlled by my parents began. Beyond the Town Hall was our Square, where they might very well be looking out for me. I began to lag. Evie's forward movement slowed. It was an impasse; and there was only one way to avoid being detected in her company.

"Well," I said, coming to a halt. "Well. Till tomorrow."

Evie looked over her shoulder.

"Aren't you going home?"

"Who? Me? I was going for a walk in any case."

Evie smiled her sideways smile.

"So long, then."

I walked smartly back to the bridge, over the top, then crouched and peeped back round a convenient angle. I saw her dress and socks ascend the street and disappear between the Town Hall and Miss Dawlish's bow window. I walked home by way of side alleys and entered the Square from the north west; but our cottage was dark and my parents in bed. I thought I would play the piano a bit before I went to bed so I practised the study; and now it seemed to contain not only Imogen, but Evie, a passionate frustration on every level.

My mother put her head round the door and smiled at me lovingly.

"Oliver, dear. It *is* rather late—"

The next day my right forefinger was very tender as if the end of the bone had been bruised. Regretfully therefore, I gave up the piano for the day and went for a walk instead. It was a long walk with a sandwich lunch and ended in the evening. There was very little time left before my pursuit of Evie and I spent it making myself as attractive as I could with the little basic material at my disposal. I could do nothing about Robert's profile and extra three inches and motor bike.

But I could remove any trace of what was called 'Five o'clock shadow', and compete with Evie's perfume by means of hairoil. I did not deceive myself into believing that I was good looking, but I had heard that girls were relatively indifferent to that. I hoped they were; for as I inspected my face in the mirror, I came to the regretful conclusion that it was not the sort of face I should fall in love with myself. There was nothing fragile about it. I tried smiling winningly at myself, but the result made me grimace with disgust.

"How much milk today Madam? Thank you Madam, yes Madam, no Madam, thank you Madam, good day Madam—"

I stuck my tongue out at myself.

"Meeeeeh—"

There was no doubt about it. I should simply have to be subtle, devious, diplomatic—in a word, clever. Otherwise the only way I was going to *have* a girl was by using a club. Evie was girl, much girl. I remembered the violence with which she had shoved me down the bank, remembered the ease with which she had put away my tentative pawings—the gentle, pleading way she had put my hands aside. I doubted to myself whether I should really get very far with a club either. Yet the evidence of the trousers sunk without trace was indisputable.

Evie was accessible.

"Meeeeeh—!"

She passed along the south side of the Square without looking across at our house this time and experience had taught me to wait for a while. She was already sitting on the coping stone of the bridge therefore when I came up with her. I was doubtful about any course of action, had evolved no brilliant stratagem. I had thought of professing an interest in bird watching in the hope that she would agree to come with me and stalk the lesser redshanked strike or whatever it was. But in fact I could not tell a barn owl from a skylark and knew myself to be entirely ignorant of the patter. As for looking for wild flowers or searching out the lines of ancient fortifications, or digging for rare minerals—No. I could think of nothing. And anyway, all Evie had to do was to hang up her parent's prohibitions like a sort of notice, and I was confined to the bridge, or the impossible route between it and Chandler's Close. In the event, what I did was to make a little dancing step in front of her and stand, my walking stick held across my waist.

"Hullo Evie!"

Evie put her head on one side and smiled up at me.

"Took you a long time."

"I was busy."

"You!"

I resented the implication.

"I'm recovering. I worked very hard, you know."

"Isn't the piano work?"

"Course not."

She said nothing, but continued to smile. I wondered vaguely what the piano was; but while I wondered, Evie began to hum. The notes drew and preoccupied me, as notes always did so that I searched my memory.

"Dowland!"

Evie laughed aloud, her face lovely and all alight. She began to sing.

" '—and daily weep
and keep my sheep
that feed upon the down, upon the down, upon the down, upon the down!' "

"You've got a jolly good voice! You ought to—"

"Used to have singing lessons."

"Miss Dawlish? Bounce?"

She nodded, laughing.

"Lah, lah, lah, lah, lah, lah, lah, lah!"

Then we were laughing together in the sodium light at the memory of our dreary teacher and her dull lessons.

"*Lah*, lah, lah, lah, lah, lah, lah *laaaah*!"

"Why don't you sing more often?"

"Not Dowland, someone else—see, Mr. Clever!"

"You should keep it up, Evie."

"Would, if I had someone to play for me."

"Haven't you got a piano?"

She shook her head. I looked past it at the river but examined instead an instant picture of Chandler's Close. Sergeant Babbacombe's cottage faced Captain Wilmot's across the entry—two cottages a distinct degree superior to the rest. Beyond them, the cottages got progressively smaller, meaner, dirtier and more decayed down to the ruined mill. Children tumbled and fought in the muddy road. The boys wore the uniform of a Poor Boy; father's trousers cut down, his cast-off shirt protruding from the seat. Mostly they had bare feet. I realized suddenly that it was what the papers called a slum. If Sergeant Babbacombe hadn't got a piano, certainly none of the others would have one.

"What about Captain Wilmot? He—"

She shook her head again.

"He's got a gramophone and a wireless. Used to ask me in when I was a kid, to listen."

"That was kind."

"Glass of lemonade and a bun. All classical music. And he's got a typewriter."

We were silent for a while.

"So I don't keep up my singing," said Evie at last. "And what with learning to type—"

I understood. I nodded solemnly. It was a shame.

"You weren't playing today, Olly, were you?"

I laughed and held up my bruised finger. She took it to examine the tip with her own white fingers; and the performance repeated itself as if we were something reproduced from a die or plate—the giggles and laughter, the change from pursued to pursuer, the lugging down into the darkness of the pier, the semisurrender face to face, denial, consent, denial, kiss and struggle, scent, three plums and a glimmering skin, vibration—

"Don't you like me?"

" 'Course I do—no, Olly, you mustn't—"

"Aw come on—"

"You mustn't—it's not nice!"

I knew and accepted that it wasn't nice; knew too that as far as I was concerned, niceness wasn't the point.

"Leave go, Olly—leave *go*!"

I was down the bank again. This time, one foot went in the river. I scrambled back up but Evie was staring into the sky.

"Listen!"

There was a faint droning among the stars. She skipped to the rise of the bridge and stood still. As if some exotic star had come adrift, a red light was moving under the shaft of the Great Wain.

"It'll come right over head."

"R.A.F."

A green light appeared beside the red one.

"I wonder if it's Bobby?"

"Him?"

Evie was still staring up, her mouth open, her head leaning further and further back. The plane became a dark shape between the lights.

"He said he'd fly here as soon as he could. Said he'd stunt over Stilbourne. Said if he could find a place to land he'd take me up—"

"I bet!"

"Oh look! It's going to—No, it's not."

She turned on her heel as the plane passed us, and lowered

her head gradually, until the shadow had sunk behind the trees of the wood.

"They wouldn't let him yet. He's only been there a week or so."

She stamped her foot.

"Boys are *lucky*!"

"I shall learn to fly when I go to Oxford—probably. I'd thought of it."

She turned back to me quickly.

"Oh I should like to fly more than anything! And I should like to dance—and sing, of course—and travel—I should like to do everything!"

I grinned at the idea of Evie doing everything; then stopped grinning as I remembered the trousers, and the one thing I wanted her to do—or let me do.

"Let's get back down."

Evie shook her head.

"I'm going home."

She began again the sliding walk, back towards the arc of street lights. I followed, cursing the R.A.F. to myself, and its latest recruit in particular. As we passed each light in turn, I felt the spheres of influence thickening round me and slowed. Evie slowed too.

"Well—so long, Evie. Until tomorrow."

Evie went on with a glint of smile over her shoulder. Looking back, she lifted her left hand by her shoulder and wiggled the fingers at me. With great care I examined the poster of Douglas Fairbanks that stood outside the cinema. When she had disappeared into the Square, I went home too, keeping to the other side of the Town Hall and not leaving its shadow until I was sure the Square was safe.

My mother was darning a pair of my pants when I got in. She flashed her spectacles at me as I sat down, then bent her greying head to the work again.

"I see young Bobby's back."

"Bobby Ewan?"

"Weekend."

"Good God—He didn't fly down, did he?"

My mother laughed and adjusted her spectacles with a glittering thimble.

"Of course not. Mrs. Ewan took the car into Barchester and met his train."

My father knocked out his pipe in the grate.

"He'll have travelled First Class. Have to. Officers do."

"He's not an officer yet, Father! A sort of cadet."

"Oh. Well. I don't know."

I got up, seeing my mother glance at me then away again. I went straight off to the bathroom and examined my mouth, but there was no lipstick on it. I stood before the mirror, confirmed in my previous estimate of my face. It was not only unfragile. It was melancholy and bad-tempered. I wondered what a naked girl looked like exactly—what Evie looked like. I had no precise idea but thought it would look pretty good. I found myself wondering the same about Imogen Grantley; and caught myself up, appalled at having even inadvertently equated the two of them. I knew I had no business thinking these thoughts or wanting these things. I was only eighteen; cricket, football, music, walking, chemistry, were what I was for. Imogen would win the subtle, indescribable competition. I leant my forehead against the little mirror, shut my eyes and stayed like that for a long, long time. Not thinking. Feeling.

With the morning however, I plotted fiercely. I played with extravagant bravura, determining that somehow I would get Evie to a place where I might wreak my wicked will. I understood it to be wicked. Well, I was wicked. I swore a great oath of implacability and felt better. After tea I walked up to the woods and searched the nearer fringes for a place of dalliance and concealment. There were enough of them; and each raised my temperature a little higher until I was sweating and panting. I went back towards the road, to go down the hill and wait for her on the bridge; and heard a rocket coming up from it. The Duke of Wellington's profile flashed by me. I had a glimpse of Evie sitting astride behind him, white embroidery shivering in the wind, eyeflash and the open mouth of delight. Then they were gone and the woods settled behind them.

After a while I walked down the hill, over the Old Bridge and up the High Street. I went indoors. My mother looked up from darning my father's combinations.

"Back early then, Oliver?"

I nodded and sat down to the piano. After a while my mother went out very quietly, shutting the door behind her. I played to the empty room, the empty reception room, the empty Square and town. I bruised my finger again.

The next morning when I went into the bathroom I peered round the edge of the window to see Robert, for I intended to cut him as pointedly as I could if he should notice me; but he wasn't there. The punchball was motionless as ever between its upper and lower attachment and the motor bike was on its stand in the corner. It was chalky all over, and even at that distance I could see the deep gouges in the metal. One of the handlebars was bent right back. I was excited immediately; and a little worried too—not for Robert but for myself. I did not like my pleasure in the sight of the wrecked bike. I even spoke aloud to force myself into the correct human position.

"Poor old Robert! I hope he's not hurt—"

Then I remembered the fluttering white embroidery, the naked knee, and my thoughts and feelings became too confused for understanding. I shaved as quickly as I could, and hurried downstairs. Breakfast was waiting for me, though my

57

father had already gone through into the dispensary. When she heard me, my mother came in to give me my breakfast.

"Seen Robert's bike?"

My mother put down the hot plate and wiped her hands on a tea towel.

"Heard about it. I *knew* that would happen sooner or later. Young men—motor bikes ought to be banned from the road."

"Is he hurt?"

"Of course he's hurt! What d'you think?"

"Badly?"

"They don't know yet. Took him to the hospital."

I helped myself to HP sauce.

"Anybody else hurt?"

My mother was silent for a while. Her silences always made me uneasy. She could see through a brick wall, could my mother. Uneasily I remembered how dark it had been under the bridge—reassured myself. There was no reason why I should not have met Evie accidentally on top of it, and stopped to chat. After all, she worked practically in the same house.

"Anybody else hurt, Mother?"

"Motor bikes aren't the only thing I'd ban!"

She gathered together the débris of my father's breakfast.

"Nobody else was hurt—more's the pity!"

I watched her under my eyebrows as she went back to the kitchen. Clearly my mother was having one of her moods. She did not have them often, but when she did, I found it necessary to stand from under. I should not get more accurate news from her today, no matter how diplomatically I probed for it. I could not question my father either; or rather, though I could question him, he would have forgotten the details already. That left Evie herself. So after breakfast I strolled through to the dispensary, where my father was working

58

silently as usual. I heard the laborious clatter of a typewriter from the reception room. It was true then. She was all right. Not hurt enough to stay away—well enough to get there on time, too. All at once I was swept up on a wave of joy. What my swung fist had failed to do to Robert, he had done for himself, without any help from me.

"Can I give you a hand with anything, Father?"

My father swung his heavy head round. There was surprise behind his pebble glasses. He tugged his grey moustache once, shook his head briefly, then swung it back again. I had some kind of intuition that my mother's mood had started very early. I went to our piano and tried to strike a mean between finger-soreness, irritating my mother, and reminding Evie that I was there. I wandered into the town; saw Mrs. Babbacombe pecking at Sergeant Babbacombe by the Town Hall, so loitered, until she had gone on. When I passed him in my turn, he looked from the mat he was brushing and nodded to me. There was no doubt about it. He had never done it before, but now he nodded to me. I gave a jerk of my head which might be taken either as recognition, or avoidance of a fly and walked on. I was so surprised that I stood for a long time before the window of the Antique Shoppe, examining the contents. I did not know what to think. I read such titles as were still legible among the tattered books, picked one out and examined it. I did not see it. I saw instead Sergeant Babbacombe's extraordinary nod—as if I were a soldier too, or drinking companion. I put the book back in the tray, went past the Jolly Tea Rooms where six college wives were eating buns, drinking coffee and clacking, past Douglas Fairbanks outside what had been the Corn Exchange and stood, looking down the rest of the High Street at the Old Bridge. There was nothing to worry about. From the High Street, anyone— any pair—against the further pier would be completely hidden. I was safe.

Mrs. Babbacombe came up the other side of the High Street, carrying a string bag full of packets and paper bags. She was wearing her usual grey suit, usual grey cloche. An enormous artificial pearl hung on her left ear. She came up wizened and smiling, with an unacknowledged greeting to this person and that. Then she saw me. She did not alter her brisk walk; but her head sank sideways, inclined, her false teeth dazzled. She held that bow, that smile, for a good five yards, till a man by a lamp post hid her.

Knowledge poured into me. Awe-stricken, I realized exactly how perilous my lust was. I knew something else, too. Neither Sergeant Babbacombe nor his wife could have my mother's flashes of diabolical perception. This was Evie's doing. She had used me as a lightning conductor. More accurately and unconsciously than I ever played any scale, I raced over in my mind the realities of people. Evie could never have Robert for keeps. She could not even catch him. If she tried, she would come up against a cliff of adamant. But since she liked his motor bike and had paid for her rides —yes, paid for them!—she needed excuses for lateness, for staying out, for—My cliff was as adamant as the Ewans's; but not as high. No, not nearly as high. It was not as high, for example, as the cliff that separated Evie herself, from the louts who hung round the Town Hall, out of work. For Evie, I was a lightning conductor. To her parents I was a possible suitor. Bellicose Sergeant Babbacombe must have been twisted by those white fingers, persuaded by that tinkling voice that we were courting. I put my hair up out of my eyes and took a deep breath. Apart from my terror at her parents assumptions, I was lost in conjectures as to how Evie had used me. Was it I, for example, who had kept her out after twelve—I who had pinched Bounce's car, even? And what else? What other strings did Evie have to her trim little bow? I assumed without thinking, that she would lie when necessary, as I lied myself when necessary. In that case, driven by necessity, she might say anything. I saw as in a nightmare, Sergeant Babbacombe turn up on our door step, twisting his three-cornered hat in his hands, and demand of my father to know what my intentions were. I knew what my intentions were, and so did Evie; but they were too neatly describable for family life. I went home, round the other side of the Town Hall, and played the piano very softly.

That evening the news of Robert was mixed. The only thing that was certain was that he would be in hospital a long time. I went out early to the bridge, thinking to myself that if I were seen sitting there often enough, no one would notice or at any rate, comment, on my meetings with Evie. It was twilight again before she appeared, pacing down the street. She came up to me with no more than a ghost of her smile.

"Weren't you hurt at all?"

Her smile became brighter, and a bit arch.

"What d'you mean Olly? What you talking about?"

"Last night."

"I wasn't—"

"I saw you, Evie. On the bike."

She shuddered suddenly, drawing up her shoulders.

"What's the matter?"

"Goose walked over my grave I 'xpect. Olly—"

"Well?"

She glanced sideways at the street.

"You won't tell, will you?"

"Why should I?"

She smiled at me nicely and let out a long breath.

"Thanks."

I laughed with fierce sarcasm.

"Oh yes! You were here with me on the bridge, weren't you? We talked about music, didn't we? We went down there by the water, fishing for tiddlers. Didn't you show your mother a jam jar full of them?"

"I just said—"

"You said I took you over to Bumstead. You said I pinched Bounce's car! I know you!" I glared down at her, trying hard to hurt. That, at least, was possible. "I wonder what else you've said. How many lies you've told. Getting me out of bed in the middle of the night—such a nice boy, Oliver, even if he hasn't got a motor bike!"

"It isn't like that, Olly—I *had* to! You just don't understand—"

"I understand well enough. You're like—" I stared round at the road, the river, the looming darkness of the woods at the top of the hill. I snatched a phrase out of the air without knowing why. I roared it. "You're like—the Savoy Orpheans!"

Evie burst into giggles that confounded me and shut me up.

"You're such a funny boy, Olly!"

Her giggles went on and got mixed up with laughter and choking. She leaned forward from the coping of the bridge, held me with both hands, her head bowed between them. I could feel how she was shaking.

"So funny! So funny!"

"Shut up, Evie! Good God! *Will* you shut up?"

At last she was silent. She pulled herself up and sat upright on the coping. She shook her head so that her bob flopped and flew aromatically. She took a scrap of white stuff from under the imitation amber bangle on her left wrist, touched her face here and there, then put the scrap back again. Despite myself, I was touched. I disguised this slight decline in manliness by being as gruff as I could.

"You were dam' lucky. Why weren't you hurt?"

"Doesn't matter. Oh all right—I wasn't on the bike."

"How the—"

"I egged him on. I dared him. He said 'This little machine

would climb a tree with me at the controls.' So I dared him. I wanted to try with him. There was this chalk pit—"

"Where was it?"

"I wanted to try too, honest I did. 'Not with you on the back, young Babbacombe,' he said. 'Hop off.' The bike fell right on 'im."

There was a droning under the Great Wain. I looked up and saw the red light moving towards us. It was some regular flight, then, some exercise or other. Evie did not look up with me. She was looking at her feet. When she spoke it was in a strangely hoarse voice, and one from far down in Chandler's Close.

"E may be a cripple."

The plane droned away, sinking slowly out of sight behind the trees at the top of the hill. Evie cleared her throat.

"For life."

Then we were silent, Evie looking down at the road between my feet, I digesting this news according to my nature. I felt properly shocked of course; on the other hand I felt a little of Stilbourne's excitement and appetite at the news of someone else's misfortune.

She drew herself up on the coping, and smiled at me.

"You didn't play today, Olly."

"Yes I did. Softly."

I held up my forefinger, in explanation and invitation. But Evie glanced at it then away. In some extraordinary way she had inhibited her exhalation. It was like one of those scraps of film run backward; flames, seen to draw themselves in, reconstitute the paper they had burned, then vanish, leaving nothing but ordinariness. Even the sodium light in her right eye was a duller and perhaps steadier gleam. This inhibition affected me too; but optimistically enough I discounted it.

"Come on, Evie! Let's go down there!"

She shook her head.

"Come on, young Babbacombe!"

The sodium light exploded.

"Don't call me that!"

She stood up quickly.

"Robert does."

"He can call me what he likes!"

"Temper!"

She seemed about to speak, but changed her mind. She squinted over her shoulder, beating any possible stone dust off her seat. I exploded like the sodium light.

"Why the hell did you come down to the bridge, then?"

She stopped beating her seat and looked at me, eyes and mouth open.

"Why? Where else is there to go?"

She wiped one hand on the other, smiled briefly and turned away towards the street.

"Evie—"

She did not answer, but went on walking. At the bottom of the Bridge where the street began she glinted back over her left shoulder, lifting her hand by it and wiggling the fingers. I stood, my walking stick across my thighs, and watched her. She was doing her walk again, our local phenomenon, nothing moving but legs below the knee, on the invisible line patrolled daily by Sergeant or Mrs. Babbacombe. She moved from light to light; and with my new craving, my new wickedness, I saw and understood how the moneyless shapes of men outside each pub watched her, their heads turning with a silent and hopeless avidity. She would be fifty yards past them, when the burst of jeering, libidinous laughter came. I knew that I should never be able to endure it myself, my feet swollen, face rigid; but Evie never faltered. I went home by way of side alleys to avoid running that gauntlet.

Next morning, shaving sullenly, I had an idea that stopped the razor on my cheek. There, in the Ewans's stable was Robert's bike. I looked out quickly and saw that nothing had been done about it at all. I finished shaving and hurried down to breakfast, telling myself I must be careful and diplomatic. Lead the conversation round, bit by bit.

I was so quick that both my father and mother were still eating. My mother broke off to fetch my breakfast from the pan. This was fortunate.

"Young Robert's bike is still in the stable, I see."

"Oh?"

"Yes. It is."

My father glanced up under his eyebrows through his pebble glasses.

"Best place for it."

I nodded, and kept the ball in play.

"It's out of the rain, anyway."

"Ha!"

My mother came back and put my plate down with the kind of firmness that always indicated further communication.

"Don't think you're going to have that bike, Oliver, either to borrow or buy!"

My mouth fell open. She sat down again.

"Besides," said my father, "We couldn't afford it."

"I've got—"

"And you'll need it," said my mother, "every penny of it."

"If Robert—"

"I *do* wish you'd clear your mouth before speaking, dear," said my mother. She swallowed. "He will want it again anyway. If his father lets him ride it again, which I doubt. Ewan's not a fool."

"How can he want it again if he's a cripple?"

"Cripple!" said my mother. "Who gave you that idea?"

"He was badly bruised," said my father. "He's broken some ribs too. But he'll be all right."

"I thought—I saw the bike—it was so badly damaged—"

"Just a few weeks," said my father. "Young Ewan's all right. Teach him a lesson, silly ass!"

"Every week you see something in the *Stilbourne Advertiser*. Killed, like as not. Oh! Which reminds me, Father— Imogen Grantley's getting married in Barchester Cathedral!"

"That'll be a big do," said my father as he pushed away his plate. "When?"

"July the twenty-seventh. Only gives her a few weeks. But of course with money to spend—"

"Lot of nonsense," said my father. "Dressing up."

"After all, Father, her great-uncle *was* Dean. He married a Totterfield. Then—I wonder who she'll have for bride's maids?"

"Not me, at any rate," said my father. He twinkled through his pebbles and stood up. "I've got work to do."

"Oliver, dear, eat your other egg!"

"Put the bike out of your head, old son. When you're as old as I am, you'll understand."

"Eat it up."

"Leave me alone!"

"Don't speak to your mother like that!"

"Leave me alone! Leave me alone! I—don't want it!"

My father sat down and looked at me gravely.

"He's up and down all the time," said my mother looking at him. He looked back. She nodded meaningly. "I always wondered if it was a good idea."

They began to weave a web across the table of care and attention.

"Routine," said my father. "That's what he needs again."

"Oh I don't know, you know. He's always been up and down you know. I was the same."

"A steady, calming routine. He ought to go back to school for the last three weeks or whatever it is."

"I won't. I'm not a schoolboy any more!"

"Show us your tongue, old son."

"For God's sake!"

"Don't speak to your father like that!"

"I want to go away."

"*Now*, Oliver—!"

"I do. Anywhere."

"Well," said my mother kindly. "You're going to Oxford, aren't you? Only a few weeks' time—"

"Storm in a teacup," said my father gruffly. "Needs a good clear-out, that's what the boy needs."

"He was always up and down. Even as a baby."

My father stood up again, and plodded towards the dispensary. His mutter was cut off by the door.

"I'll just go and get him a—"

I stood up too, my legs trembling.

"Where are you going, dear?"

I slammed the dining room door brutally. I stood, still trembling, looking at our battered piano with the worn music stool before it. I swung my left fist with all my force into the shining walnut panel between the two brass candle-holders and it cracked from top to bottom.

"*Oliver!*"

I was wrestling with the chains and locks and bolts of the front door.

"Oliver—come back! I want to speak to you! All because we won't buy you a—"

I slammed the front door too, and heard its immediate replication from the church tower. I got our iron gate open, and stood on the cobbles by the chain rails round the grass.

I saw Mrs. Babbacombe carrying her inclined smile at me along in front of the railing before Miss Dawlish's house.

I only came to myself a little when I was sitting on the coping stone of the Old Bridge. My throat was drier than it had ever been and my left hand looked like a boxing glove.

I began to wander aimlessly round the town. I saw, from far off, Evie leave the Ewans's house after surgery and hurry back to Chandler's Close; and sneered to myself. But then I saw her come back, past the vicarage, and vanish down an alley that led to Chandler's Lane behind our garden. Still jeering and sneering at myself I went another way round, to see where she had got to, but Chandler's Lane was empty. I began to search it, without hope; but searching was something to do.

So strong is habit, even in as small a place as Stilbourne, that the last time I had been to the farther end was when I had been pushed in a chair as a small child. There was a wooden hut at the dead end on a piece of waste land, huddled under the slope up to the escarpment. I examined it curiously for I had never seen anything like it before. It was a Roman Catholic Church, and the notice outside said that Mass would be celebrated there whenever possible. This made me smile, despite my storm, for I had never met the Roman Catholic Church outside a history book. To come across it living, so to speak, was like finding a diplodocus. I began to laugh. Evie came out of the hut. She had a duster in one hand and began to flap it vigorously.

"Hullo, Evie!"

She glanced round, saw me, and caught her breath.

"I'm busy."

I laughed again, jeeringly.

"I can wait. Got nothing to do."

"Oh go away, Olly! Unless—"

"Unless what?"

"Nothing."

She went back inside. I stood, examining the notice, the carved figure and sneered. I was fixed in a sneer.

After about twenty minutes, Evie came out again, brushing the front of her skirt down. I noticed that she had tied her silk square over her hair. The celebrated, the notorious cross hung outside her cotton dress. She paid very little attention to me but locked the door behind her and set off to walk back to Chandler's Close as if I were no more than a bush.

"You been having a Mass or something, Evie?"

She gave a little laugh and walked on.

"You wouldn't understand."

"Come for a walk, then."

"No."

"Ha! No motor bike."

"I been helping him as much as I can!"

"*You* can't help him! What d'you think you are? A nurse?"

Evie said nothing but smiled a secret smile. She dropped the cross down inside her dress. I watched it disappear, with a sudden feeling of absolute determination and certainty.

"You don't need to help him, anyway. He's all right. Only bruised and a few ribs broken."

Evie stopped, turned and faced me. I stopped too.

"What d'you mean, Olly? You mean he's better?"

Bitterly, I felt the unfairness of it all—Robert getting a reputation for daring and all this sympathy and paying nothing for it. Evie was looking at me, through me, with a face of heavenly delight.

I spoke out of my certainty.

"Help *me*, then."

I glanced at the bushy track that led winding up the face of the escarpment. I turned back to her, and nodded solemnly.

"Yes. He's all right. I'm not."

"And he won't be—"

"I'm not."

Evie moved to go home. I caught her wrist as Sergeant Babbacombe had caught it and bore down on it, so that she stopped, staggered, then stood looking up at me.

"I'm not. You think you can do what you like, don't you?"

I walked to the beginning of the track, towing her.

"Olly! What you doing?"

I went on towing. The bushes and scrubby trees closed round us. I towed her up the steep path, not looking round.

"Little Olly isn't a sucker any more. Little Olly is in charge from now on. And if Bobby gets better and starts anything, little Olly will break his neck."

"Let me go, Olly!"

"And little Evie's neck."

She laughed her scandalized laugh and pawed at my swollen knuckles with her free hand. I shook it irritably. The path got narrower and the trees closed in over it. Evie's hand relaxed and hung limp from mine. She no longer pulled back, but followed obediently. I laughed aloud.

"That's better!"

"Listen, Olly. I got to explain."

I answered her elaborately.

"No explanation is necessary, my dear young lady!"

"What I'm trying to say is, everything's different—see—if you could only—"

"Here we are."

I looked round me at the clump of trees, hardly hearing Evie's voice as she went on talking. The edge of the escarpment concealed us from the town; and beneath the trees was a tangle of undergrowth, sown thick with flowers. I drew Evie round from behind me, and we were facing each other.

"You haven't been listening!"

I put my arms round her and squeezed with that strange

feeling of certainty. Her eyes closed, her head went back. I lowered my own and kissed her. She resisted me for a moment but for a moment only. Then she pulled her mouth away with a shocked giggle and tried to escape. To my surprise, that strength for carrying coal and chopping wood now seemed wholly inadequate.

"Let me go, Olly! I got to help Mum!"

I squeezed again, bore her back against a tree. She was solid and female and I did not know how to go on. Then, with primitive inspiration I took out the rigid and burning root of the matter and laid her unresisting hands on it. Evie's eyes opened and she looked down. Her mouth went lopsided and instead of a smile there appeared a sneering grin, that was at once knowing and avid and contemptuous. Her voice was a hoarse and breathy mutter. Her chest started to go in and out.

"Should I have all that?"

Yes, I assured her, breathy and hoarse as she, so that the wood swung with it and jumped with heart-thump, yes, she should, she should. Her legs began to give, she was sliding down me. And through all the turmoil I heard her breathe at me.

"Get on with it, then."

The clump settled back into place as my heart settled. I was lying flat, eyes half-open, and the leafy tops of the trees were out of focus. Each heart-thump shattered them like an image in suddenly disturbed water. I was aware of nothing but peace; peace in my blood and nerves, my bones, peace in my head and my deep breath and in my slowing heart. It was a good peace, that spread. Those were good leaves up there, with a good, bright sky beyond them. This was a good earth beneath my back, soft as a bed and all its unexamined depths was a good darkness. I let my head fall sideways and saw a white sock and brown sandal. The other was a yard away. I turned over and got on one elbow, and examined her feet and legs inch by inch in a deep, calm peace. My eye searched them, parted and slack, white, soft, gentle with wandering veins of faintest blue. It searched further, calmly past her thighs to her almost hairless body, where the evidence of my perilous onanism was scattered round her pink petals. It moved along, taking in the white arms on either side, hands open, to the shiver of pulse over her heart; inspected where she breathed, more quickly than I, so that the two smooth segments of spheres with their pink tips, bounced and quivered minutely, for all their firmness.

Triumph and delight began to burgeon and spread in me. I looked, smiling at the cotton dress, rucked, jammed up in a bundle from armpit to armpit. I lifted my chin and stared, laughing into her face. Her head was propped up a bit, eyes dark and deep and slitted between the shivering paint-brushes. Her lips were everted still more, her mouth breathing quickly as if it were the only way she could rid herself of her body's heat. I sat upright and she gave a quick glance at me from far back in her head, then looked away again.

She muttered.

"That's all I s'pose."

Her dark hair lay strewn among the smashed and scattered bluebells. I bent quickly, and kissed the nearer pink tip and she shivered from head to foot. I kissed the other, laughing, then sat back and put the hair out of my eyes. As I did it I felt some discomfort, so lifted my left hand again and examined it. The knuckles were a mess, the whole thing puffed and ungainly. When I tried to flex my fingers, the pain stabbed up my arm.

"My God. I wonder why it's begun to ache like this? It wasn't aching before!"

Evie lifted her head and examined herself.

"Got what you want now, haven't you?"

"Here. Have my handkerchief."

"Ta."

Possessively I reached to her breast, but she smacked my hand away.

"Leave me alone!"

She jumped up, and pulled at her dress so that it stretched down like a concertina.

"Look at all these creases—how am I—Oh!"

She stamped in the brown leaves, snatched her head square and her knickers from where I had thrown them.

"You've got some leaves in your hair. And a twig."

"*Look* at these creases!"

They certainly told the story explicitly enough. I had a passing thought that Evie must surely have met this particular difficulty before, at least with Robert. I tried to help her, passing my hand heavily down her back, but she jerked away.

"Don't think I belong to you, young Oliver!"

"I'm older than you are!"

She looked at me, not glinting or provocatively, but as a human being might look at an object. It was odd, I thought, how dark grey eyes can seem to be. She opened her mouth to speak, but shut it again and went on, smoothing and beating. Nevertheless, I thought—and the triumph that had been burgeoning, burst into sudden scarlet blossom—I had *had* this sulky, feminine, gorgeous creature!

"Hold still a moment, Evie. I'll get the twig out."

I untwisted her hair, smelt it, and the scent of the earth, and the faint, thin smell of the smashed flowers. I threw the twig away and hugged her. She was a sullen and passive lump in my arms.

Evie pulled away and picked among the trees towards the path. I followed. She began to walk faster, hurrying out of the trees, down between the bushes, broke into an uneven trot that she only interrupted where the brambles were too close together for anything but delicate negotiation. A few yards from Chandler's Lane I stopped her.

"Evie—"

She looked up at me, smouldering.

"When shall we—"

"Don't know."

"Meet you here this evening."

She smiled at that, a little of the lop-sided grimace I had seen once before.

"No fear."

"Tomorrow then."

"How should I know?"

"Tomorrow—after surgery. In the evening."

"Want to bet, Mr. Clever?"

I took her firmly by the shoulders.

"Tomorrow evening after surgery. I'll be waiting for you. We'll have some more—"

She said nothing but stared darkly through my chest.

"Shan't we, Evie? I said 'Shan't we?' "

Evie drooped a little between my hands.

I watched her slide, at her accustomed pace, past the vicarage and the cottages, down towards Chandler's Close. I stood there, in the pride of possession, enjoying her bob, the swell of her seat and the little motion of her delicate arms. I went home and faced the music. There was plenty of it and all the more powerful for being muted. My father treated me with a serious concern that was as fearsome as open anger. Nobody mentioned the split panel of the piano. My mother thought I ought to be ashamed; but with such a desperately concealed fear for my sanity that it was very obvious to me. My father examined my hand, painted the cuts with iodine, and gave me some opening medicine. I apologized all round of course, saying I had not known what came over me. I would mend the piano or pay for it to be mended somehow

74

when I could. I would not offend again; and yes, I felt perfectly *calm*. And once more, I was desperately sorry. But really, nothing touched me, not the smashed panel, nor my father's deep anxiety. Not even my mother's tears.

That evening when I went to bed, my left hand jumped and throbbed. I put it outside the bedclothes to cool it; and then, finding that not much relief, I propped my forearm on the pillow so that my hand was above my head in the air and some of the blood drained from it. It was extraordinary how different life had become. Even the thought of Imogen, though she caused me my usual pang, brought no more than a covered one, a pang with the point blunted. I pinned the memory of a scented, white body over it. I found myself wishing strange things, wishing that Imogen might know I had *had* Evie; that she might see—but she knew of course—how pretty was our local phenomenon, this hot bit of stuff through which I had achieved my deep calm. I found myself envisaging Stilbourne with college gents to the east, stable lads to the west, a spread of hot, sexy woodland to the south of it and only the bare escarpment to the north. Chandler's Close to the Old Bridge—a silver thread, a safe, patrolled line; but Robert had tapped the line with his motor bike by way of side alleys; and I, the even safer thread between the Close and her wooden, ridiculous church. I had, in terms of set book, cuckolded Sergeant Babbacombe. I was a bit vague about cuckolding, but it seemed the right word. Most of all, I returned to her body, enjoying it again in detail. I knew about the details now. I began to plan new triumphs. Tomorrow, with careless grace and ease, I would weave a chain of kisses from one pink tit to the other, laughing, and enjoying the shivers and the tremors of my possession. Hand throbbing above my head, head filled with white femininity, it was after dawn, before I fell asleep.

75

The next day lingered even by breakfast time—stretched ahead an unendurable length. It was hot and bright and I could not think how to pass the time of waiting. My parents were still grave and anxious; so to make what amends I could I behaved as considerately as possible, helping with the washing up. I asked what I could do—shopping, perhaps; but my mother would not have it. When I went into the dispensary and asked my father if he would like me to deliver medicine—a thing I had not done for years—he merely shook his head. I could not go for a walk; for the opening medicine proved effective and powerful so that for most of the day I had to stay close to the house. Nor, with my swollen hand, could I play the piano. My father had taken the front off and put it in the dispensary against the wall so that he could mend it when he had time; and now when I sat on the music stool I was confronted not by music but by intricate works. This did not matter to me, though, and I was not particularly anxious to play. I did no more than try out with my right hand the chromatic scale of which I was proud because of its extreme velocity. The piano did not seem to have suffered much. Or rather, this last blow was no more than an additional damage to an instrument already punch drunk. Even the keys seemed to wear the ghastly yellow grin of someone determined at all costs to see the funny side of his own predicament and go down, game to the last.

Surgery was not yet over by the time I was pacing to and fro in Chandler's Lane but I was impatient. I walked by the hedge of clipped veronica, leaned for a while against the high wall at the bottom of our garden. I looked up at the slope to the escarpment with its cascading rabbit warren, its alders, and beyond them my clump of sexy trees at the top. I heard the church clock strike the hour and my heart thumped at the thought of Evie leaving the surgery. But Evie did not come. I waited with growing anger—walked almost to Chand-

76

ler's Close itself, but saw no Evie. Back and forth I patrolled on my silver thread and I could not leave it; knew gradually that I was stuck on it and should stay there if I had too until day had drained away if necessary, all night if necessary—should stay as long as there was the remotest chance—

Then just when I had begun to think the chance was remote indeed, I saw her coming. She was being our phenomenon again and exhaling more than ever. She paced, and smiled, mouth open. She was glad and excited to see me for when I lifted my hand to her she laughed, tossing back her dark hair, and broke for a step or two into a run. Her scent came with her.

"Hullo, Evie! You've been a long time!"

"Been having my lesson."

"Lesson?"

"You know. Secretarial."

"Oh! Old Wilmot—"

Evie giggled and turned into the narrow path up to our clump without any compulsion. She glinted—or "flashed" would be a better word—over her shoulder and I followed close.

"Short—'and. Short-hand."

"How d'you spell 'pneumonia'?"

Evie laughed aloud and broke into her girly run until the slope of the path stopped her.

"Nothing like that!"

The shrubby trees closed in. A breath of air pulled itself through the leaves between her dress and me and a cloud of scent from the honeysuckle enveloped us both. I picked my way after her, keeping close.

"What d'you mean 'Nothing like that?'"

"Not medical things. Well—"

She laughed again.

"He just picks up any book."

77

The brambles slowed us. My nose was a very few inches from her hair. I did not know whether I was smelling the mixed enticements of summer, smouldering in the hedges that now met over us, or the scent of her body. Whether I could smell it or not, I could see how her body moved under the thin white and blue cotton. My own body rose. I caught her arm and pulled her round and kissed her hard. She took her mouth away, laughing.

"No, no, no!"

She pushed me away, laughing and flashing and breathing scent, and ducked on up the path.

"He said he'd have to beat me if I didn't do any better!"

I roared with laughter at the thought of Captain Wilmot, heaving himself out of his electric chair and grinning like a wolf.

"If he could catch you—'Fix bayonets!'"

"He said I'd like it."

"The old sod! You ought to tell your father!"

Evie laughed too but on a higher note. We broke out of the path into the clump. I made a grab at Evie, but laughing still, she girly'd away among the bushes.

"Evie? Where are you?"

Silence, except the town noises from the valley under us. I blundered through the bushes and she was waiting for me, flushed and shining. I put my arms round her and she shoved with both arms.

"No! No! No!"

Clear, up from the town came the clangour of a brass bell and the outline of a raucous shout.

"Hoh yay! Hoh yay! Hoh yay!"

Evie caught her breath. Before my eyes, two buttonlike projections rose in the thin stuff over her breasts. She pushed against me, pawing, eyes shut.

"Take me, Olly! Now! Have me!"

And a minute later, flat among the flowers, cotton dress

78

huddled up, eyes shivering, face twisted, changed from laughing—

"Hurt me, Olly! *Hurt* me—"

I did not know how to hurt her. As I beat my hasty tattoo in boyish eagerness, I was lost among the undulations, the contractings and stretchings of her body. She would not consent to any quick rhythm; only the long, deep ocean swell in which her man, her boy, was an object, no more: and this deep swell of an apparently boneless woman was accompanied by a turning away of the head, both eyes shut, forehead lined—a kind of anguished journey, concentrated on reaching a far spot, dark, agonizing and wicked. I was a small boat in a deep sea; and the sea itself was a moaning, private thing, full of contempt and disgust, a thing to which a partner was necessary but not welcome. I could no longer direct; and my boat was overwhelmed by waves, suddenly controlled by her, driven towards the rock, where a cry rose, loud and tortured, and I was among the breakers, ship-wrecked—

The trees settled back into place. The only thing that seemed to make a noise was my heart. The flowers were still and remote as if they were painted. I got away from her quickly and lay with my face in dead leaves. A cold apprehension was settling on me and turning slowly to something worse. I heard her stagger to her feet and busy herself with her dress. I pulled myself to my knees and stared at her but she ignored me. She turned towards the path but I ran and got between her and it.

"Evie!"

She blundered sideways through the bushes and I went after her and caught her arm.

"Damn you, Evie!"

Then we were face to face, I shouting and she screaming as to whose fault it was and why and how, almost as though by making a noise we could put off some moment or other.

And then as suddenly as we had begun, we fell silent again; and the irreparable fact made itself felt in cold, silent menace.

Evie turned away, picking her steps among the trees towards the edge of the escarpment as if she needed air. I followed her, absurdly making as little noise as I could. I cleared my throat then whispered.

"D'you think you'll have a —?"

She shook herself irritably and smoothed out some horizontal creases with unnecessary violence.

"How the hell should I know?"

"I thought—"

"Well you'll just have to wait and see, like me, won't you?"

She looked at me with her unpleasant, lopsided grin.

"Thought you'd got something for nothing, didn't you?"

I stared back, my teeth clenched, hating the whole female race. As if she could read what was inside my head, she muttered at me.

"I hate men."

A faint, brazen ringing came from the valley. We both turned to look. Sergeant Babbacombe had reached his second station. Between the alders, I could even see him, a tiny spot of red and blue, on the crest of the Old Bridge. Evie looked away from him. She was standing in front of me and a little to my right side. Her arms were folded under her breasts, legs straddled, head slumped. She was not a local phenomenon. She stood like a washerwoman. Slowly, she searched the town, from the church to the bridge, from Chandler's Lane right across to the other slope up to the woods. When she spoke at last, it was the crude voice of Chandler's Close, right at the other end among the ragged children, a voice hoarse and bitter.

"And I hate this town—I hate it! Hate it! Hate it!"

I looked down, past the brown cascade of the rabbit warren, down the green slope to the town itself. I examined the high wall at the bottom of our garden, our grass patch, the bathroom window. I looked over the roof to Miss Dawlish's house, heard the matter-of-fact honking of a car. Down there, the depth of my offence was to be measured. I drew back, under the alders. Evie turned to me with a sneer.

"Don't worry. Nobody'd recognize you at that distance."

"Evie—what're we going to do?"

"There's nothing we can do."

"Couldn't you—"

I had the vaguest idea of the biological factors involved, and no resource. I whistled ruefully to myself and put back the hair out of my eyes.

"When will you know?"

"Next Monday or Tuesday—perhaps."

She turned away from the town and began to thread through to the path. I followed, and neither of us said anything. The evening was very bright, and still warm. Perhaps it was the sight of her back, so slight and helpless, her bare arms so weak, that struck me with a sudden realization of what a dreadful thing it was to be a girl.

"Evie—"

She stopped, without looking round.

"Cheer up. It may never happen."

She gave a kind of sob and started running down the path. I followed more slowly, wondering what to do. When I came out of the path into Chandler's Lane she was thirty yards away and going home. She was pacing again, contained and secure.

I went home, confounded at the sight, and unnerved at my peril. I remembered Oxford with an awful pang. If—*if*—she had her baby, it was goodbye to Oxford. I could hear the whispers and titters coming out of the very bricks and mortar.

Left school at eighteen to get married. Had to. Or if not, it would be seven and sixpence a week—maintenance. I knew about seven and sixpence. It was one of our snigger-triggers, like monthly, or nine months and a whole dictionary of others.

"It may never happen!"

Then, with great force, the thought of my parents hit me. My father, so kind, slow and solid, my mother, tart, yet with such care of me, such pride in me—It would kill them. To be related even if only by marriage, to *Sergeant Babbacombe*! I saw their social world, so delicately poised and carefully maintained, so fiercely defended, crash into the gutter. I should drag them down and down through those minute degrees where it was impossible to rise but always easy to fall—Yes. I should kill them.

I tried to sneak upstairs but it was no good.

"Oliver! Is that you, dear?"

"Yes, Mother."

"Hurry up and have your supper."

I went through into the dining room. They were both sitting at the table. I looked at the cold ham. I had forgotten about food, and did not want any.

"I'll skip it."

"Nonsense!" said my mother glittering, at me. "A growing lad like you! Sit down, there's a good boy. Besides, Father has something to tell you."

I sat down obediently and stared at the slices of ham on my plate.

"What are you waiting for, Father? Tell him!"

My father finished his mastication, his eyes thoughtful, the ends of his grey, walrus moustache moving gently up and down. Then he turned his bald head slowly in my direction.

"It's about the piano, Olly."

"I said I'm sorry."

"That's all done with," said my mother, laughing gaily. "Quite, quite done with. Over and done. Listen!"

"We've been thinking. It'll take a long time to repair. Glue would have to set—and so on. But that hand of yours'll keep you off it for weeks I should think—"

"Get *on*, Father! You're always so slow!"

"Now you've never had a proper present for working so hard. So we thought, your mother and I, we'd get them to take the piano into Barchester and recondition it. Two jobs at once. Money's tight, of course—isn't it, Mother?"

"Money's always tight—that's money!"

"But I've been into it a little, and I *think* we can just about—"

"And if your hand's better in time you could always start playing the violin, Oliver, you used to play so beautifully before you went mad on the piano!"

"Then when you come back from Oxford for the holidays, you'll have a proper instrument."

He turned back to his plate and went on eating.

"Of course," said my mother, "it won't be a BBC piano you know!"

"Be better, though," said my father. "They can do a lot. It not as though it's a wooden frame after all. Wooden frames always go. I don't know why they use them."

"Perhaps they can even get the keys white again."

"Wooden frames always go. It's the climate."

"We don't need the candle holders. They can take them off."

"Iron frames give you a steady tension. Ours is an iron frame."

"What's the matter, dear? Now come on! It's all forgotten and done with!"

"Steady on, old son!"

"It's The Blood you know, Father."

"Show us your tongue old son."

"Don't bother him. Eat some ham, Oliver. That'll do you good."

My father got up ponderously and plodded into the dispensary.

"Why, you old crybaby," said my mother gently. "I know how it is, dear. Growing up is difficult even for boys. It's the blood, you see. Everything stirred up. Now eat your ham dear and you'll feel much, much better. Why, I remember— you'd be surprised, Olly. We're really very proud of you, you know, my dear, only it wouldn't be good for us always to be telling you about it. Here's the mustard."

My father came back silently and put a little glass down by my plate. In it was some more opening medicine.

The days dragged themselves away. Mrs. Babbacombe continued to flash me her brilliant sideways bow from any distance up to fifty yards. Evie did not walk the patrolled route any more. When I waited in Chandler's Lane it was with less and less hope. Sometimes I could hear her typing in the reception room, and sometimes I saw her making her quick way from surgery to her home, but that was all. Evie was avoiding me. Monday came, Tuesday and Wednesday, and she made no sign. I had settled from terror to a state of continual worry. My dreams had a new dread; and always the same thing. I dreamed I was walking about Stilbourne, but condemned to death. My parents were in the dream—indeed all the people of Stilbourne were there and all concurred in the death sentence since my crime, which the dream left vague, was unpardonable. I would wake up with relief to find it a dream; and then remember Evie.

A week later I saw Evie again, though not to speak to. I was in the bathroom and caught sight of Evie and Dr. Ewan's weedy partner, Dr. Jones, walking up and down together on the larger of the Ewans's two lawns. I stared at her first, anxiously, as if I had X-ray eyes; but could make out nothing different about her. Indeed, if anything, she was more the same than before. She was moving only below the knee, her matted, unruly eyelashes were flickering, her mouth was open, lips smiling mysteriously and exhaling. I was at once indignant and relieved. Surely a girl in her condition—if she was in her condition—But weedy Dr. Jones was behaving strangely. His hands were clasped behind his thin body. He would warp his knees away from her, look down sideways and laugh. He didn't look much like a doctor, I thought; more like a silly old man—forty if he was a day.

Then I remembered that whatever he looked like he was nevertheless a doctor; and I knew why girls saw doctors. I watched the happy pair disappear back towards the house as if they had been gorgons. One thing was clear. I had to see her. Yet I had no excuse for going through into the reception room. Unless I had something as obviously wrong with me as a broken arm or a rash, any plea that I needed medical attention would be met by my father with more opening medicine; or perhaps, in view of the complete success of the last two doses, some closing medicine. Even my left hand had healed and limbered up, as though busting the panel of a piano were only a sort of eccentric fortissimo and all in the day's work. Melancholy and anxious, I surveyed myself and found myself healthy. There was no doubt about that. Moreover I had a veneration for doctors which was remarkable, seeing how close I lived to them; and I had an irrational fear of their tests as if Dr. Ewan might gaze into my Specimen then announce that I was an expectant father. I had to see her, and braced myself to be blatant about it. I went and took a book from the shelf by my bed, marched downstairs, straight into the dispensary. My father was peering through his pebble glasses at a prescription.

"Book for Miss Babbacombe," I said casually. "Thought I'd take it through. Save me the trouble of—"

I need not have worried, for my father went on peering and muttering without noticing, as his right hand groped for a spatula. I strolled along the passage and opened the door into the reception room. Dr. Jones leapt away from Evie as if she had stuck a hypodermic in him. He stared at me, a minute trace of lipstick visible by his mouth. He said with a kind of relief—"Oh it's you!"

Then the outer door banged open and massive Mrs. Dance trundled in, wailing as loudly as her weight and breathlessness would let her. She had young Duggie in her arms. He was red in the face and jerking about. Dr. Jones changed immediately and took charge.

"Calmly Mrs. Dance! Let me have the child. Miss Babbacombe—I need you."

They bundled through into the surgery, all four—or five—of them. I was left by the door, holding out my copy of Miss Sitwell's *Bucolic Comedies*. I turned away, still racked by uncertainty as to whether I was expectant or not and went through the dispensary where my silent father was making his slow, utterly sure movements.

So I returned to spying and prying and patrolling; and however my mother tempted me to eat, I had no appetite. Then it was Sunday morning and I met Evie again. I was standing glumly by the wall at the bottom of the Ewans's garden, in Chandler's Lane. I had even prowled round the wooden hut at the other end for I thought they might have been doing or having their possible Mass; but the place was silent and shut. I had gone the other way, past the bottom of the vicarage garden and the cottages with their hedge of veronica, until I was well within sight of Chandler's Close itself. I had hung about there, hoping to see her come out of the cottage at the entrance. At last I had wandered back, nagged and hopeless, and stood, leaning against the rough brick of the Ewans's wall. I glimpsed at first a flutter of skirt coming round the long corner. I knew it instantly for Evie's cotton dress, white, and strewn with the pale blue sprigs of flowers. I jumped away from the wall and went towards her quickly. She was not pacing, but moving as quickly as I was, hair blown back, dress moulded against breast and thigh, one knee going past the other. I went straight up to her and grabbed her by both arms.

"Evie—tell me!"

She stared up at me sullenly as if I were her enemy. She was made up heavily and carefully. Her matted lashes had been combed out, then stuck together with some black stuff so that they were like plates. There was blue stuff round her eyes, and her lips were so neatly painted they looked like scissor'd slips of scarlet paper.

"Leave go, young Olly. I'm not going to see you again."

She wrenched at my grasp but could not shift it. I whispered urgently.

"Are you going to have a baby?"

"Oh that!"

I shook her.

"A baby! Are you—"

She got free and stood, looking venomous.

"You'd like to know wouldn't you?"

"I must!"

She shook her bob irritably and made to pass. I stretched out my arms to stop her. She tried to duck under them, then finding this no use, ran sideways into the path up to the clump. She saw where she was and turned, but I was blocking the entrance. She hurried up the path away from me but I followed closely. I grabbed her bare arm and swung her round.

"Evie!"

87

She turned her head towards the hedge and spat out something.

"Look, Evie—what's the matter with you?"

She straightened up and glanced at me under her black, clicking plates.

"Swallowed a fly."

"Once and for all. *Are* you going to have a baby?"

"No I'm not. A fat lot you'd care if I did. Or anyone."

"Thank God!"

She mimicked me savagely.

"Thank God, thank God, thank God!"

She stumbled on up the path, smacking branches aside, careless of nettles, ducking and weaving. I trotted after her. A great joy and peace had opened in my heart. I trotted faster, was no more than a yard behind her as she stumbled on with movements at once slack and jerky. As she ran, she talked, the words jerky as her movements.

"You wouldn't care if I was dead. Nobody'd care. That's all you want, just my damned body, not me. Nobody wants me, just my damned body. And I'm damned and you're damned with your cock and your cleverness and your chemistry—just my damned body—"

We broke out into the sunny clump. Laughing in my joy and freedom I pulled her round again, wanting her to share it, wanting everyone to share it. One arm at her back, her rounded breasts against me, I lifted her face with my hand to kiss it. She grimaced, turned it sideways and spat like a kitten.

"Come on, Evie pet! Cheer up! Cheer up, young Babbacombe!"

For answer, she collapsed against me, hands on my shoulders, head sideways on my chest. She spoke and choked and snivelled.

"You never loved me, nobody never loved me. I wanted to

88

be loved, I wanted somebody to be kind to me—I wanted—"
She wanted tenderness. So did I; but not from her. She
was no part of high fantasy and worship and hopeless
jealousy. She was the accessible thing. I waited smiling for
these sheets of summer lightning and storms of summer rain
to fade away so that we could come to sensible terms again.
She was, after all, a girl, this curious, useful, titillating
creature; and sure enough, after a while her snivelling
stopped. I expected an arch, mysterious smile to come back,
with a little teasing, but instead, she pushed herself slowly
away from me and shook out her hair. She went slowly
through the thickets to the alders above the rabbit warren,
doing things to her eyes and nose with a scrap of handkerchief. She threw herself down in the shade, leaned on one
elbow and stared moodily at Stilbourne in its frame of leaves.
A moment or two later I came and knelt close behind her,
cheerful as a bee at a flower. I stroked her bare arm and she
brushed off my hand as if it had been a fly. Laughing, I
flicked up her skirt with a Rabelaisian gesture; giggling I
grabbed the elastic band of her knickers. She jerked away
from me when she felt my hand and they came down to her
knees. With one electric convulsion she got them up again
and was staring at me over her shoulder, make-up struck on
a dead, white face.

Some things need no study, no learning, no repetition in
pursuit of memory. They burn themselves into the eye and
can be examined ever after in minute detail. Moreover it is
their nature—since we cannot even think, without leaving
a mark somewhere on the cosmos—to bring with them their
own inescapable interpretation. Kneeling there, then, staring
at her, and not seeing her but only the revelation, the pieces
fell into place with a kind of natural inevitability.

Captain Wilmot, with his wolf grin and load of unexca-
vated shrapnel! Fix bayonets! Captain Wilmot, good neigh-

bour, chasing the ghost of the youth that had been blown out of him, a desperately dedicated teacher with a naturally gifted pupil!

She had knelt in front of him, that was plain to see; and he, lowered on to a chair perhaps, had reached forward over her bowed head and struck with his right hand, raising those red welts it may be in time with some long ocean swell: and then, tiring—for he was not strong, this broken, heavily secreting gargoyle—he had struck those weaker blows with his left hand across the other weals.

I cannot tell how long I stared at her without seeing her, both of us motionless and silent. I was eighteen and so was she, and I think my first sound was some kind of a laugh, a laugh of sheer incredulity. Then I could see her again, eyes and lips stuck on a white face, Stilbourne out of focus below and beyond her. I laughed again, out of incompetence, feeling lost, as if I or someone had come to a gap, a nothingness where it was not just that the rules were unknown but that they were non-existent. A slice of life.

Keeping her eyes on me, watching me from the back of her head under the motionless plates, Evie put one hand up to her hair and gave a laugh that did not rearrange her face. Then she was silent, still watching me eye to eye, and the blood burst into her face. It was no ordinary blush, glow, suffusion. It tightened the glistening skin, swelled and immobilized the face, seemed to hold her mouth open. She spoke hoarsely, defensively, yet as compulsively as she had blushed.

"I was sorry for 'im."

I looked away from her, down at the town. Made brighter by the shade under the alders, it was full of colour, and placid. I looked at our wall, the bathroom window, the window of the dispensary, our little garden—and there were my parents, standing side by side on the grass. I could see how my father stood, looking down at a flower bed, while my mother bent in her active way from the waist and picked among the flowers. They were too far off for me to recognize them by anything but their surroundings and their movements, my father a dark grey patch, my mother a light grey one. All at once, I had a tremendous feeling of thereness and hereness, of separate worlds, they and Imogen, clean in that coloured picture; here, this object, on an earth that smelt of decay, with picked bones and natural cruelty—life's lavatory.

The object was still staring at me and her face was white again. We had made so little movement, so little noise, that a blackbird came picking over the humus. It only had one leg, and was making do, flirting its tail sideways to keep its balance.

Evie knelt up, and the blackbird fluttered out of sight.

"Olly—"

"Yeah?"

"You won't—"

"Won't what?"

She sagged on her arms, looking down at the earth. She glanced up again, biting her lower lip so that a tiny stain of crimson appeared on each incisor.

"I'll do anything. Anything you want."

My heart gave a heavy leap and my flesh stirred. They were down there, the two grey patches and she was up here, life's necessary, unspeakable object. I stared curiously at my slave.

"How long? I mean—when did it start?"

"When I was fifteen—"

Unbelievably, a faint smile appeared under the make up, a faint smile in her white cheeks as if she were remembering something shymaking but good.

"—off and on."

I reached out my hand but she flinched away.

"No. Not today—I—I couldn't!"

She got carefully to her feet. I addressed her firmly.

"Tomorrow then, after surgery. I'll be waiting. Up here."

She shook herself, braced herself; and was Evie again. She even contrived to exhale a bit, and smile lopsidedly. Then she picked a path through the undergrowth and disappeared.

I stayed where I was, among the growth and the smells, and stared at Stilbourne, that framed picture hanging on some wall or other.

At supper that night, my mother announced a plan.

"You could get yourself tea, couldn't you, Father? For you and Olly? Or perhaps Olly could—"

My father looked up.

"What? Why? When?"

My mother's spectacles flashed.

"There now! You've neither of you been listening to a word I've said!"

My father sheepishly composed himself into an attitude of attention.

"All right, Mother. I was thinking. Yes. What was it?"

"And *his* mind's miles away! I must say—"

"What was it then, Mother?"

"*As* I said," she announced with dignity, "I'm going into Barchester. On Saturday."

My father rubbed his head, and identified Barchester in his mind.

"Oh yes."

"I shall catch the one o'clock bus. The wedding isn't till three."

"Wedding?"

My father identified weddings.

"Whose wedding?"

My mother set down her cup with a clatter. Clearly, it was a mood-day.

"Whose wedding do you think? The Pope's? Imogen Grantley's of course!"

After a time I could hear them again. My mother was concluding a lengthy speech.

"I shall have tea at the Cadena."

"Yes that's the best place, I suppose."

"What d'you know about it, Father? You've never been there! I might go to the pictures afterwards."

"There's a cinema in Stilbourne, Mother," said my father, eager to help. "I don't know what's on, though."

"There's a lot you don't know," said my mother tartly. "Right under your nose, some of it."

My father nodded placatingly.

"I know. Perhaps Oliver would like—"

"*Him*!" She referred to me as if I were a contemptible object in Australia. "He'll be traipsing about the countryside, I'll be bound!"

For a time we were all three silent. I could hear my mother tapping her shoe against the table leg.

"So I'm not asking either of my fine men to escort me—"

The tapping stopped. She paused, then completed her sentence with brooding finality, "—because I know it wouldn't be any good."

My father and I looked at our plates, silent for different reasons.

Even by teatime next day, my mother was still smouldering; and I, with much to conceal, had nervous thoughts that jumped into downright apprehension when she broke into our silence.

"That girl was a long time in the dispensary, Father!"

"Yes. Yes, she was."

"Well I hope you gave her some good advice. It's time somebody did!"

My father wiped his grey moustache and nodded soberly. People occasionally came to him for advice. This, I believe, was because he looked more like a doctor than Dr. Ewan did, and had not the awesome aura of Dr. Ewan's county status. People could *talk* to my father, they said; and indeed this was true, since he seldom answered them. Chewing the cud of an idea until he had extracted the last possible juice from it, he would appear to listen to them as they rattled on. This gave them an impregnable sense of his wisdom; and indeed, since he was effortlessly good and kind and methodical and slow, he may have been wise too. My special relationship as a son, made it difficult for me to judge.

"What did she want, then, Father?"

The cynical end of me triumphed for an instant over apprehension and saw my father offer Evie some opening medicine. But he was staring at the teapot and pursing his lips. I waited.

"She doesn't think much of—people."

I debated with myself whether asking what girl this was would convey my indifference; and decided sensibly against. But my mother was glittering and nodding meaningly.

"And that doesn't surprise me! It doesn't surprise me at all!"

"Beasts," said my father. "All men are beasts. That's what she said."

"*Well*," said my mother. "What d'you expect from a girl like that? Men are what you—"

I blew tea all over the table cloth. This small crisis was a great relief; and by the time my back had been thumped I hoped the subject might be changed. But I should have known that my mother in this strangely extended Mood would not be content with a word or two only; and that my father would have to comply.

"Go on then, Father. What did you say?"

My father wiped his moustache, passed a hand over his baldness, adjusted his glasses, and stared at the teapot again. I could hear my mother's foot begin to tap.

"I said 'No'."

The tapping went on, and my father heard it. He amplified.

"I said no they weren't. I said—*I* wasn't! I said our Olly here—"

The tapping stopped. My father was gleaming and glinting sideways at me.

"I said that he had his faults of course, lots of them; but he wasn't a beast."

Then there was a pause. My mother looked straight at him and spoke in a still voice.

"What did she say?"

My father had turned back from me and was looking at his plate. He answered her vaguely.

You know how it is, Mother. I get to thinking, and they—I can't remember."

My mother stood up, took the teapot and marched with it into the kitchen, banging the door to behind her. There was another pause; then my father spoke to me, softly.

"It's the wedding, you see. After she's been to the wedding, she'll be—better."

By the end of surgery I was waiting in the clump. Evie was late, but still she came, cotton dress and all, strolling up the path. I had pictured her in my feverish lubricity, humble and anxious and aware of her new status. But Evie was smiling, triumphantly, if anything, and she was exhaling again. She walked past me, securely, went through the bushes, through the alders, and sat down among the scrapes at the top of the rabbit warren. I hung behind, looking from her to the town and back again.

"Come back here, Evie!"

She shook scent out of her glossy bob and lay back in the

95

sun. She stretched her arms wide, stretched her legs down together and the cotton dress rearranged itself. She laughed at the sky.

"Come on, Evie!"

She shook her head again, and tinkled a laugh, girlishly. I went and squatted by her.

"Look—what's the matter?"

Evie turned on all the works, glinting at me and flickering her tangle of eyelashes. She sank her chin, stretched even further so that the top half of her body lifted away from the earth and I caught my breath. There was scent in it.

"Let's go in the clump—and have some fun!"

Evie shut her eyes and collapsed. She lay like that, unsmiling.

"Here, or nowhere."

"But—that's the town!"

She lifted her head and stared at it, grinning on one side of her face.

"So it is—Mr. Clever!"

I cajoled, ordered, pleaded. Evie would not budge. She lay slack, unsmiling, stretched out and answered me always with the same phrase.

"Here or nowhere."

In the end I fell silent and stared moodily at the brown earth and the dry pellets of rabbit dung. Evie got up and picked things off her dress.

"Evie—tomorrow—"

Tomorrow was the day of the wedding. I knew already what I should need, to stick like a plaster over the thought of it.

"See you here—in the afternoon."

Evie smiled sideways at me.

"Of course, Olly. Why not?"

Then she went away, secure and perfect as a ripe nut.

It wasn't until we were all three at the table and having an early dinner so that my mother could catch the bus into Barchester, that I understood. My mother was amiable and excited and talked as much as her food would let her.

"—and you needn't worry about that girl any more, Father. She's going away!"

"Oh?"

"Going to her aunt at Acton. She's been promised a job in a firm. They import timber, I'm told. A good thing too!"

"Good thing?"

"For her, I mean."

My father masticated, gazing heavily before him. He wrinkled up his brow and shook his head.

"London. I don't know. It's a long way; and a young girl—"

He went on masticating and shaking his head forebodingly as if he were envisaging an endless line of young girls throwing themselves off London Bridge.

"Nonsense, Father!" said my mother, glittering and laughing. "She's going to stay with her aunt!"

My father changed his shaking to a nodding, masticating slowly meanwhile, thirty-two times, or it may have been sixty-four. My mother stopped laughing and glittering and stared at the wall. When she spoke, she used something like the voice with which she announced her unnerving, her diabolical perceptions or intuitions; a voice matter-of-fact and basic, as from someone not quite my mother; but now, elated, even gay.

"Provided she's careful, she'll have no end of a time!"

I did the washing up, in an incomprehensible rage. I went out after I had finished, striding through Stilbourne away from the escarpment. I dived into the sexy woods, turned aside and broke out into fields again. It was said you could see the very tip of Barchester Spire from the crest of Pentry

Hill and I circled the whole thing, before I climbed to the top. But there was a blue distance where Barchester and its spire might be. I turned round, moodily following the escarpment with my eye to our furry clump; and there was a tiny white speck at the top of the brown warren.

No fear! No *bloody* fear!

I went by way of Cockers, past the Racing Stables, through the fields of Little Farm, and climbed again. The white speck was still there. You could see it from half the county. I began to run clumsily along the edge of the escarpment, past Ansdyke and the Barrows, over Iron Gate and the Devil's Hollow. I came thudding to the clump, the sweat running down my face, my hair smeared into it; and from the town I heard the church clock strike three.

"Evie!"

I collapsed beside her, my heart beating against the raw earth. She was sitting up, her legs crossed, her hands supporting her on either side. Stilbourne and all the spreadout county were shaking beyond her as if they had been running too.

"Evie—please!"

"Here or nowhere."

I felt the eyes of Stilbourne on my back; but they were distant, they wore pebble glasses and we were two inscrutable specks. It was an irrational fear and embarrassment that laid a hand on my flesh but a real one. Evie understood this, laughing sideways triumphantly, so that I think even she was astonished and frightened, when I put one hand round her back, one on her breast, and savagely stopped her startled speech with my mouth. She neither resisted nor co-operated; and afterwards, when I was gasping face-downwards, she went away flushed, silent and ashamed.

I stayed where I was, and at last looked down under my arm, trying to recognize the odd figure that moved here or there, almost beyond the edge of seeing. I got up and went crouched through the alders and only straightened up when I was down in Chandler's Lane. I opened our front door as quietly as a thief. I debated whether I should not get out my violin and play at the gipsy music my mother so astonishingly urged me to practise. I thought I might play softly at first, then more and more loudly so that my father would never know exactly when I had come in—or even that I had been out at all. But I had a more immediate urge for reassurance, so I went to the dispensary and walked in casually. My father was standing by the long bench under the window. The top half of the window was open to the clump. He had not yet bothered to replace his binoculars in the leather case that hung behind the door. They stood by him on the bench, battered but serviceable. My mind did a simple sum. Magnify by ten. Ten into six hundred yards goes sixty times. Sixty yards.

There was a book on the bench before him. He shut it slowly, turned, came past me without looking at me. He took his white lab coat off a hook, put it on, and went as slowly back to the bench. He took a prescription off the wire file and peered at it closely. He looked up at some bottles then back at the paper. Suddenly he crumpled the paper in his hand and leaned on his knuckles, his head bent. There wasn't a sound.

At last he straightened up, smoothed out the prescription carefully and took down a bottle. All at once I knew what was going to happen, could feel it happening, unstoppable as sex. I felt it in my shuddering, in the confusion of Imogen and Evie and the piano and Robert and my mother; in the fierce and fruitless struggle between my will and my hot eyes. I gasped out my oaths, half-strangled.

"Damn! Damn! Damn! Oh—damn!"

Furious and anguished and helpless, the water not falling, but jetting on my shoe, on the bench, on my hands—

"Damn! Damn! Damn!"

Head up, hands clenched, window elongating glossily, the dark underground lakes broken up, flowing and flowing—

"Damn! Oh damn—"

My father was turning his head from side to side as if it had been tied with elastic ropes and he an animal, not knowing how he had been caught.

"I had to know, you see—*had* to. After what she—" He put the bottle down, glanced at the window, then at his hands; passed one of them over his bald head. "Laughing and laughing. Hysteria, I thought. Laughing and laughing and—or sneering."

I stayed where I was, settled in misery, wickedness and defeat, wondering already what corner there was I could hide in, never to be seen again. My father cleared his throat and went on, in a voice curiously determined and strained by the determination.

"Young men don't—think. I—You don't know about that place, Chandler's—Yes. Well. There's—disease, you see. One's not suggesting that one's necessarily—been exposed to infection—but if one goes on like this—"

He took off his glasses and cleaned them with surgical care; and suddenly, for all his professed but indifferent agnosticism the voice of generations of chapel burst out of him.

"—this man what d'you me call him—these books— cinema—papers—this sex—it's *wrong, wrong, wrong*!"

I stood, a heap of dung, yearning desperately for some sewer up which I might crawl and reach my parents, kneel, be forgiven, so that the days of our innocence might return again. I stood, watching him make up prescriptions for all the ailments of Stilbourne.

After that I stayed indoors and played my cheap violin in place of the piano, hoping to do at least something that my parents wanted. I avoided Evie as if she had been one of the diseases my father had talked about; and indeed I saw her only once before she went. I was standing by the sitting-room window, my violin in my hand. I had played the passionate gipsy music with extreme care; and now stood, staring across at Bounce's house, thinking ruefully how much she would have approved my dutiful practice, when Evie came along on the other side of the Square. My mouth opened slowly. This known, this detected, this fallen woman, had not changed in any way at all. Lips everted, mysterious smile, pert nose, glossy bob, knees motionless, she slid along, and as ever, bore the almost palpable aura of sex in the air round her. I watched her till she slid out of sight beyond the Town Hall. She was wrong, wrong, wrong; and so was I. I went back to my violin, to the extravagant oportamenti, and throaty vibrato of my gipsy music.

So Evie disappeared; but it was years before I found out why. I was not the cause, though with a mixture of vanity and shame, I thought so. Nor was Robert with his motor bike, nor Captain Wilmot with his typewriter and braided whip. Duggie Dance might have been in the convulsions that killed him and Mrs. Dance wild with grief and hysteria, but she had two Stilbourne eyes in her head and a Stilbourne tongue in her mouth. What ejected Evie from our midst, in the direction of London Bridge, was the tiny smear of lipstick at the corner of Dr. Jones's mouth. That was too much. Evie went, and the coloured picture of Stilbourne was motionless and flat again.

Yet Evie avoided London Bridge for I saw her once more, and in Stilbourne. It was two years later in the autumn and I was on the verge of my third year at Oxford and restless with the world since anyone could see a war was only just round the corner. I did not think I should complete my third year, and bleakly enough, saw myself walking into the barrage of another Western Front. Stilbourne Great Fair was on, that annual event which brought what small business the town had, to an exasperated stop. The fair was so old-Saxon, perhaps—that only a special Act of Parliament could have abolished it. Stilbourne's exasperation was all the greater, since what had once been a row of stalls set up in the curved High Street, between our Square and the Old Bridge, had become a riot of swings and roundabouts and mystery rides and tunnels of love and chairoplanes, the only object of which was the sale of pleasure. It was Saturday Night. The sky was clear and moonlit and cold; but the steam from the competing machinery—that vast disharmony of a thousand pipes—had built up in pillars and mushrooms over the fair and the lights from flares shook down from them as though a war had already started. For three hundred yards were ranged the shooting galleries, roundabouts, sideshows, crockery—smashing, three darts for sixpence and a dip in the lucky bran tub. The lines, the gaudy flowerbeds of bulbs pulsed with the generators and the naphtha flares of the smaller stalls made the whole place bounce and quiver. One pavement was free, and it was by this route and this alone that one could escape from the fair and the clouds. I had returned, with a sophisticated nostalgia to assure myself that I could no longer enjoy the pleasures of childhood, and was finding with a mixture of irritation and amusement that I was in danger of enjoying them thoroughly. I strolled, hands in the pockets of my grey flannels, scarf heavily wrapped and hanging down behind and in front, along the free pavement. Here, the crash, the blare, the mechanical musics, the shouts and screams, thump of a wooden ball against a canvas screen, or pang of a bullet against an iron sheet were a little to one side, as if one had partly dissociated oneself from them. The pavement was empty, for it was still too early to find lovers standing in the alley openings or behind the tents; and drink had not yet fouled the pavement with spew. Just beyond the outclassed lights of the cinema I saw a girl coming down the pavement towards me. I could not mistake the bob, the motionless knees and demurely pacing feet. It was natural, after all, that I should see her again. Quite recently, Sergeant Babbacombe had emerged from the Town Hall in his picturesque uniform, rung his brass bell; bawled "Hoh yay! Hoh yay!" and burst before he could get the third O yay out. There was hardly room for us to pass each other. She stopped in front of me, smiling in the reflection from the pillars of steam.

"Hullo, Olly! What are you doing in this *ghastly* place?"

"Stroll. Just a stroll. And you?"

"Long weekend. I'm meeting some people."

"I'll leave you, then."

I made to pass, though I did not want to. She stayed in front of me.

"Where you going now?"

"Home. This *awful* shambles!"

"I'll walk with you."

"I thought you were meeting some people!"

She put her hand up to her bob.

"It's the sort of thing one says—"

Then we were silent, constrained, and looking each other over. London had done much for her. It was only an eighth of an inch here, a tailored curve there, a matter of material and cut, I suppose. It was a new kind of gloss; sophistication. She was wearing a severe suit of dark green, and brogues. Her hair was abandoned, yet under control—designed in its abandonment. In one thing, if only one, I was an expert and could read what I saw. Evie had hitched herself up a couple of degrees on our dreadful ladder.

"I was sorry about your father."

Evie bowed gravely.

"Have you got a car yet, Olly?"

So much for the Sergeant.

"Us? No." I grinned down at her. "Take a look at me! I'm expensive!"

Evie laughed and exhaled a bit.

"You look so solemn in glasses!"

Deftly she reached forward with both hands and tweaked off my spectacles. The night blurred.

"Hey! Damn it!"

"That's what I do to my boss when—Now you look like young Olly again."

"Give 'em back, will you? I can't—"

"All right. Keep your hair on."

She came up close, scented and solid, and fixed the supports behind my ears. I caught my dedicated breath as if it had been reminded of something unconnected with the Inert Gases. Evie moved back again.

"Bobby used to take Bounce's car."

"Well. I'm not Bobby, am I?"

"No. I see that."

The paintbrushes flickered. She turned, pacing up towards the Square, and I followed at her shoulder.

"D'you still play the piano, Olly?"

"Now and then. Haven't much time, you see. D'you still sing?"

"Who? Me? Whatever for?"

We reached the Square. Evie looked at it, then stood facing me.

"What d'you do with yourself, Olly?"

"My dear Evie! I couldn't possibly explain—"

All the same, I did. I spoke of an idea that had entertained me as if it were already actual. Crypton is inert, they say. But if one teased it sufficiently, a matter of temperature and pressure, a spark gap in a sufficiently dense cloud of crypton and another element—One might produce entirely unnatural substances, if the word was admissible. Now crypton—

Evie looked up at me, her eyes wide.

"Well, well, well. Old Olly! You *are* clever!"

I was surprised and pleased. Unquestionably London had done a lot for Evie. I had a wild thought of showing her round the labs, but dismissed it, since my status there was not precisely as high as I had suggested. The wildness spread, as I glimpsed our cottage next to the doctor's house and I even thought of inviting her in. But commonsense immediately reasserted itself.

"Oh I don't know! As for you, Evie—you're looking pretty good."

She exhaled all round us both, in the sodium light.

"Have you got a girl, Olly?"

Smiling, I shook my head, then pressed my cheek where there might be a spot coming. Evie's reply was astonishing. She nodded solemnly.

"You're still a bit young for it, aren't you?"

"I'm older than you are!"

I thought for a moment, feeling the money in my pocket, and decided on the only possible compromise in this situation, since I did not want to lose Evie at once, her exhalation and admiration. While I was thinking, Evie revolved on her heel, searching the Square. She came back to my face.

"There must be *someone*!"

"What d'you mean Evie?"

"Someone alive!"

It was a frivolous remark, I thought, with the fair going on behind us.

"We could go and have a drink—"

Evie opened her purse and examined it; but I reassured her. The money for next term was in my account already. I was wealthy, not yet having discovered the truism that

105

money cannot be spent twice. Together we went towards the Crown. I held the main door open for her and it closed behind us with a soft thump, cutting off the noises of the fair. Here, in the entrance hall, there was no smell of oil and food and sweets and sweat, no flares or pulsing lights; only the respectable smell, faint but all-pervading, of dust and linoleum. We went through into the saloon bar, crossed the Axminster carpet and sat ourselves by the bar on the high, varnished stools. Mrs. Miniver was coiled behind her arms and the counter, staring at a dim view of Edinburgh Castle. She uncoiled briefly in a professional welcome, gave Evie her scotch and water and me my pale ale, then coiled up again. I looked round me. The last time I had been in the Crown was with Mr. De Tracy nearly two years before, a notable occasion. Now, four town councillors were armchaired round a low table in the far corner and arranging something about next week's meeting. A man and woman were sitting in the other corner, saying nothing and watching their drinks glumly.

"Cheers, Olly!"

"Bung ho."

One of the town councillors limped slowly away to the gentleman's cloakroom.

Yes, I *did* have a spot coming. I fingered it in a long silence.

The town councillor limped slowly back again. As he passed Mrs. Miniver, he made some grunting remark about the weather. She uncoiled with a bright laugh, then coiled up again.

Evie grabbed her glass and drained it.

"Same again please, Mrs. Miniver!"

"Here, Evie—let me—"

"No."

The councillor who had limped back, leaned forward in his chair, one hand cupped round his ear.

"Ay? Speak up, Jim!"

"So long as we don't let the contract go elsewhere!"

"Oh. Ah."

Evie pressed her hands on her cheeks, shook out her bob, then turned to me.

"We had some good times, didn't we Olly?"

I laughed automatically. Evie drank some more scotch and water, then spoke with a kind of determination.

"Yes. We did. Good times. And now—coming back—"

I finished my pale ale and looked at Evie's stocking'd legs. They were all right. I held out my empty glass and Mrs. Miniver filled it. Pale ale was all right.

Evie went on talking.

"People one's been brought up with—boys and girls—together—"

She exhaled in my direction, at once arch and wistful. I laughed, and took a long drink of pale fire. I remembered things, too, and had a vague feeling that this evening might be led.

"And Robert, Evie! Don't forget Robert—"

Evie's wistfulness vanished into archness.

"Bobby! My first sweetheart!"

I drank some more, thought of Miss Dawlish's two seater and choked.

"Same again, Mrs. Miniver, please!"

"—and me."

Evie was silent, staring into the mirrors behind the bar. She was all right.

"Tuesday."

"What d'you mean, Evie?"

"I go back on Tuesday." She flashed her smile sideways at me. "Hold my breath till then." She snatched her glass and drained it. "Same again, please!"

"Cheers."

107

"Have to look people up, first of course."

"You? What people?"

A gorgeous idea occurred to me. I grinned at her.

"How's Freddy Wilmot keeping?"

Evie said nothing for a time, staring into her glass. She drank, and put it down.

"I've just come back from Sweden with my boss."

I put an extra meaning into my grin.

"And what's *he* like?"

"David's a dear. Everybody says so. I'm devoted to him."

She giggled suddenly. Within ten seconds she had changed to something impish, not arch, Evie of the Old Bridge.

"He's good at everything. *Everything*!"

The tall stool moved under her so that she grabbed the counter.

"Whoops!"

"Cheers—"

"Let's go and pay your parents a visit."

"Come off it, Evie!"

"Or Dr. Jones—now there's a man! We could call on them!"

"I don't think—"

"No wonder Stilbourne has so many pubs. How else—I wish David was here. 'Nother whisky please!"

"Good at everything."

Evie gave a loud giggle.

"He's very good in bed. Everybody says so."

I was not going to be outdone in sophistication, warmed as I was by my flames of pale fire.

"And is he?"

But I was still nowhere near knowing Evie.

"Yes he is," she said. "He's better than you are."

The grumbling conversation from the corner stopped.

There was a hush. I got half off my stool and did a kind of dance by the bar.

"We've never been to bed," I said with a laugh about as natural as a plastic box. "Never! Come off it, Evie!"

"Never been to bed," she said nodding. "Never out of it after half-past seven. Cheers!"

I raised my own glass, laughing; and made my great Stilbourne mistake.

"Bottoms up!"

Evie put down her empty glass very carefully on the counter. She looked into it as if she could see a fly there or something. The glum couple nodded to each other, got up quickly and went away without a word. Evie made a half-gesture as if she were about to put back her bob, then dropped her hand again. She looked sideways at me along the bar, looked round the silent room, stared through the walls at the town. The lopsided sneer appeared.

"It all began," she said, "when you raped me."

A nightmare singing started in my ears. There was nothing to say—no plain statement that would bear the indisputable imprint of truth. And indeed, what had I done, we done? The four town councillors got up as one man and made for the door, past an uncoiling and coiling up Mrs. Miniver.

"Up at the top of the hill," said Evie, loudly, and circumstantially. "In the clump."

"I didn't!"

"Never stood a chance," said Evie. "I didn't want you— I was only just fifteen."

The door of the saloon bar closed. We were alone. I felt the Stilbourne tide again, but this time not whispering and tittering. The waters roared clear over my head. I slammed down my glass and flung away, to stand outside in the sodium light by the corner of the Town Hall. Evie appeared at my side, laughing; and with an effort, I kept my hands from her neck.

"Old Olly!"

"You've done me, haven't you? Done me properly, now!"

"That's right."

"And you've done yourself!"

She giggled.

"What, both of us?"

"And all you can do is laugh and laugh and—"

"Lil' Audrey. That's me."

She swayed forward towards me, exhaling; but the quarter moon and the sodium lights of the square were all that lit her. She was corpselike in complexion, her eyes and mouth black as liquorice. Rage misted my spectacles.

"Oh—go to hell!"

Evie was still for a moment. Then she began nodding solemnly.

"Ah." She said. "That. Yes. Well—"

She turned away, still nodding, then stopped. She turned back.

"Olly—"

"What?"

"I'm *sorry*! But—"

"Bit late."

All at once she became a washerwoman again, face thrust forward, little fists clenched. "*You!* Aren't you ever going to grow up? This place—You. You an' your mum and dad. Too good for people aren't you? You got a bathroom. 'I'm going to Oxford!' You don' know about—Cockroaches an'—Well. Tuesday. Never come back. Not if I can help it. So you can go on telling an' laughing, see? Telling an' laughing—"

"What the devil d'you mean?"

"Telling."

"What about?"

She breathed the words in my face with hate.

"Me 'n' Dad."

She turned away and began to walk unsteadily across the Square. She was past Miss Dawlish's bow window before her feet were under control. I stood, in shame and confusion, seeing for the first time despite my anger a different picture of Evie in her life-long struggle to be clean and sweet. It was as if this object of frustration and desire had suddenly acquired the attributes of a person rather than a thing; as if I might— as if *we* might—have made something, music, perhaps, to take the place of the necessary, the inevitable battle. So strong was this feeling, despite my fury, that I cried out to her in the empty Square.

"Evie!"

She was pacing again; and since the fair made it probable she could not hear me, I was tempted for a moment to follow her, even into the dark jaws of Chandler's Close. But I saw a light switched on in my father's cottage and the shadow of my mother pass across the curtain. I also saw—or thought I saw—a flash of the eye from Evie and fingers wiggled over her left shoulder. Then she was gone. I went home confounded, to brood on this undiscovered person and her curious slip of the tongue.

At the end of my first Oxford term I came back to Barchester by train, then took the bus out to Stilbourne. I had hung about in Barchester, scarcely knowing why—mooning round the cathedral close, or browsing in the bookshops, until I saw from the clock that if I did not hurry I should miss the last bus; so I caught it, and hid myself in a book. It was as though by this means I might prolong something. The 'something' could not be Oxford. Chemistry had engulfed music, and was regarded, I found to my surprise and indignation, as a full-time job. It left me little leisure for the indulgence of my private vice of music, though interesting enough in itself. Moreover I was eager to see my parents, exhibit the fashionable width of my grey trouser legs and tell them all about everything. Evie was gone, Imogen married; and I was a proper student with a proper sense of values and duty and therefore no worries.

All the same, I concentrated on my book.

After the old landfall
Comes the new windfall
Length without breadth
Position without magnitude
Prayer without tears.

It was no use, I couldn't understand him however good he was. I was a scientist with one private vice. I was expecting too much if I thought myself clever enough for two. I put the book away and braced myself for whatever it was, until in the darkness the bus heaved itself with a cowlike sway over the Old Bridge. I carried my two suitcases from the bus stop to our cottage and found it in darkness. While I was groping for the key under the mat I heard my mother's voice coming through the Square from the Town Hall. She embraced me with great affection and enthusiasm; and before we were properly settled indoors I understood what was up, for my father was carrying his violin in its black, wooden case. I, as it were, stepped right back into a piece of understanding as by nature, for when my father switched on the light I saw that my mother was wearing her best grey dress and gold brooch and a faint pink flush under each cheek bone. She was laughing and glittering and excited. I did not need my father's violin, nor his dark grey suit to tell me that Stilbourne Operatic Society had achieved its biennial or triennial resurrection. I believe it was always a time when my mother came to some quite extraordinary level of life. She had cornered the piano; and with the bandmaster from the college OTC on the trombone, the incumbent of Bumstead Episcopi with his double bass, a type-setter on the viola and my father as first and only violin, she controlled a theatre orchestra. The tenuity of this orchestra was not explicable only in terms of talent or its lack. If we had had more people who could play instruments we should have had no room for them. The same inadequacy limited the size of cast and chorus; so that *The Country Girl, Merry England, Lilac Time*, and *Chu Chin Chow* operated in very reduced circumstances. But even if we had had a mass of talent and a vast stage, orchestra pit and auditorium, there would still have been an overriding limitation, the social one. No one of the college's closed society was available; and Sergeant Major O'Donovan helped us only because he was right on the fringe of it. Then again, at least half of Stilbourne's population was ineligible, since it lived in places like Chandler's Close and Miller's Lane, and was ragged. Though Evie sang and was maddeningly attractive, she would never have been invited to appear, not even as a member of the chorus. Art is a meeting point; but you can go too far. So the whole thing had to rise from a handful of people round whom an invisible line was drawn. Nobody mentioned the line, but everybody knew it was there.

The SOS rose from a vein that wandered through society beneath the surface. We had no ritual except mayoral processions. We had no eloquence, no display. We were our own tragedy and did not know we needed catharsis. We got our shocked purging from *The News of the World*. Yet every now and then, the vein became inflamed by pressure and we stirred uneasily in our sleep. The SOS, laid to rest after the last performance, would wake and lick its wounds. There were many; for after a performance, few of the cast would speak to each other again. With diabolical inevitability, the very desires to act and be passionate, to show off and impress, brought to full flower the jealousies and hatreds, meannesses and indignations we were forced to conceal in ordinary life. Casting a light opera removed half our potential at a stroke, since there were always three or four people who thought themselves so insulted by failure to get the hero or heroine's part, that they withdrew their services; or worse still, sulkily accepted minor roles and embarked on a career of theatrical sabotage. By the end of our three nights' run, the other half of the cast would have been so mortally affronted they would vow never to subject themselves to such humiliations again. It was for this reason that the SOS did not perform annually. A certain period was necessary for scar tissue to form. The strife would die down, enemies return to a nodding acquaintance; and then, just too late for the next year's performance, the vein would begin to ache again. A committee would assemble, revive the society, inspect the damage done last time; then announce that the SOS, in aid of some charity, Dr. Barnardo's perhaps, would present such and such a musical in the Town Hall. Directly I saw the pink flush on my mother's cheeks I knew that I should not have to say anything about Oxford. My mother was exalted and would do the talking.

"What is it this time, then, Mother?"

"We'll have some tea, I think," she said. "Put the kettle on will you, Father? My goodness, I'm quite—It's very good, you know Oliver. I don't think we've ever done anything as good!"

She hummed a bit, then laughed.

"What's it called I mean?"

"The *King of Hearts*. Some of the music is very pretty. You'll like it."

"I'm not going. No fear."

"We'll talk about that later," she said. "D'you know dear? This time we've got a professional producer. Have you heard about him at Oxford? Mr. De Tracy. Mr. Evelyn De Tracy. I'm sure you've heard of him!"

"Well I haven't."

"He's a *charming* man! He's taken all difficulties in his stride. You'd think a professional—"

"Difficulties?"

"The Mayor's Parlour, I mean. Mr. De Tracy just said

'Well boys and girls, we shall simply have to do a little re-routing.' That's all. Just that. Father, you've forgotten the strainer!"

"What about the Mayor's Parlour?"

"Would you believe it! He said 'No.' And ever since, it's been locked."

"But surely you can't—"

"Mr. De Tracy hung the cyclorama eighteen inches further out and arranged for the cast to go that way."

"But *why*?"

"You may well ask. Here you are, dear. Father, I believe you took the kettle to the pot! You see, Oliver. It's his daughter. *Her* nose was out of joint I can tell you—"

"She's *not*—"

"She is!"

"No!"

"I'm telling you, Oliver. So you see."

I saw indeed. The Mayor's daughter, Mrs. Underhill, was a fixture. Many years before, she had appeared for a season on the professional stage and had a trained voice. Ever since, she had been our permanent *ingénue*, which simplified things. I had seen her in Persian trousers, Chinese trousers, Elizabethan skirts. Her voice could fill Drury Lane and made our tiny Town Hall seem no more than a boot box. Indeed, coming down from the woods towards Stilbourne I had once heard a high C of hers and had thought it was a patient in the nearby hospital. If Mrs. Underhill had been ignored by the committee, it was logical that her ancient father should refuse the use of his parlour; natural too that he should delay the announcement until it inflicted the maximum damage.

"How d'you manage?"

"The stairs at the back, of course. They tell me it's an awful squeeze. Back stage left," said my mother, proudly relishing the technicality. "Just the one entrance. Anyone coming on

116

stage right goes along behind the cyclorama. You can see it quiver a bit sometimes."

"More than sometimes," said my father. "Young Johnson nearly put his elbow through it, tonight."

"But how—I mean—"

My mother understood.

"Well. She *is* nearer sixty than fifty, dear, and all good things come to an end, don't they? It's time she stepped down and gave way to a younger person,"

"What part is she playing then? A witch or something?"

"You don't suppose Elsie Underhill is going to play anything but the lead, do you? My dear Oliver! She withdrew from the production. It's been a thing, I can tell you. Some people say that Claymore didn't handle it the right way—"

"Claymore? He's still the lead then—"

Norman Claymore, owner and editor of the *Stilbourne Advertiser*; and now the husband of Imogen. My heart lurched, as I understood who was the ingenue displacing Mrs. Underhill.

"They make a very pretty pair, dear, even if Mr. Claymore's voice is a little on the light side—"

"He sounds like a gnat."

"And I suppose one must admit that he really doesn't look much like Ivor. But Mrs. Claymore—Imogen Grantley that was—now *she* really looks like a princess!"

I could believe it; and tried mentally to retire to Oxford again.

"Her voice," said my father, "is—"

"*Now*, Father! Have another cup."

I knew that Imogen sang. It was perfection heaped on perfection and I made a mental note to go for a very long walk next day, lest I should hear her and be hooked again.

"I bet it's a jam on those stairs!"

"Well of course, in the orchestra we don't get to know

117

much about the circumstances back there. You'll be able to tell us, dear."

I nodded absently, still thinking about Imogen. Then—

"*What* did you say, Mother? Me? Stairs?"

"It's very near the beginning, dear. There's a scene—"

"Hey! Wait a minute!"

"You haven't heard what I'm going to say, have you?"

"Look—"

There's a scene; I think it's in Hungary or Ruritania or somewhere. It's a restaurant, you see. *She* doesn't know he's the king in disguise and *he* doesn't know she's the princess of Paphlagonia in disguise. It's very clever as an idea. I don't know how he thinks of it!"

"I'm not. No. I warn you, Mother—"

"And of course a gipsy plays to them and it's then they fall in love—"

"No!"

I noticed that my father would not look at either of us but was inspecting his cup as if he were reading his fortune in it.

"Just imagine," said my mother. "*He* plays and they have this most *moving* conversation and after the king's given him a purse of gold he goes out; and very softly the orchestra takes up what the gipsy played and he—the king I mean—starts to sing at the table close to her"—and my excited mother began to sing, with immense passion—"'Morning is dawning, dear child, in my heart—'"

"I won't!"

"Now, Oliver," said my mother, her passion calming, "don't be trying. We've had young Smith as a gipsy with silk strings and father playing for him but he's no good. He simply can't move his bow in time with the music. So I promised Mr. De Tracy. For the last performance tomorrow, I said, my son Oliver will be glad to play—"

I grabbed desperately at a straw.

"Look, Mother! I don't play the wretched instrument nowadays! And I couldn't learn anything for tomorrow if I tried."

"You don't have to, dear."

"What does this gipsy do then? Carry a music stand and Augener's Edition round with him?"

"It's that music you were playing before you went up to Oxford," said my mother. "You remember how much you liked it, dear, because you played it *all* day and *every* day for three weeks! I thought you played it very nicely."

I opened my mouth, then shut it. I looked accusingly at my father but he was still inspecting his cup. I looked accusingly at my mother; but she was placid again, smiling and triumphant.

On Saturday morning, next day, I went resignedly with my mother to the Town Hall. We entered from the big doors at the west end, and three people were waiting for us. Mr. Claymore and Imogen were seated at a small table on the stage. I was mercifully saved from an official introduction because when I followed my mother who was walking busily up the hall, the latch of my violin case came undone and I spilt the lot on the floor. Retrieving this took me all my time, so that I was standing, bow in one hand and violin in the other, before anyone paid any attention to me. I looked at Imogen and she gave me her wonderful crinkly smile but said nothing because Mr. Claymore was talking, with his voice that sounded always to me like a finger nail scratching frosted glass.

"He's here, Evelyn. We shan't need to do more than run through just that bit of dialogue, shall we?"

I thought hazily at first that this itself must be part of the play because the figure that emerged from the wings on my left was in costume.

119

"Mr. De Tracy," said my mother. "This is my son, Oliver, Oliver, dear, this is Mr. Evelyn De Tracy".

Mr. De Tracy bowed very low but did not say anything. He simply smiled down at me from the stage and waited. He was very tall and thin. He wore check trousers without cuffs and a jacket so longskirted it came almost to the knee. He also wore a wing collar and a black stock above an embroidered waistcoat. I wondered what such a figure was doing in Hungary or Ruritania. It was good of him to act as well as produce.

But Mr. Claymore was getting restless, which was surprising on a Saturday morning. He went to press on Thursday night. My mother turned to me.

"Are you in tune, dear?"

I got round the green baize curtain that separated the orchestra from the audience and took an A from the piano. While I tuned, Mr. Claymore talked to Mr. De Tracy.

"Shall I do this, Evelyn, or will you?"

I noticed then a curious thing about Mr De Tracy. He shook. He did not alter the expression on his long face which always wore a moony smile, an invariable smile with lips slightly parted, but his long body shook, three or four shakes and was still again. This shaking included his legs, which had a tendency to move sideways at the knee.

"You, Norman, I think. What a professional you'd have been!"

Mr. Claymore swelled.

"Just to save you trouble, Evelyn old man."

"And an old pro like me is always willing to learn, Norman. You have an undoubted flair."

Mr. Claymore smiled with gratification.

"I don't deny that I've sometimes wondered—However. Let me think for a moment."

He thought, receding chin on white hand. Mr. De Tracy

continued to gaze down on me with his moony smile. His eyes were large and like a pair of old billiard balls, with minute pupils so that the balls seemed both to be marked for Spot. His hair was gone on top except for a tiny black tuft that was trained slanting back. His smile was enigmatic and friendly.

Mr. Claymore sat up.

"Righty ho! Hop up here, laddy!"

I climbed on the platform and stood within a yard of Imogen.

"Now here's the scene," said the gnatlike voice. "You see wealthy customers and you steal your music closer and closer until you're playing—*here*. You can play the umpty-tum bit until *I* speak. *Then* you have to cut right down, getting softer and softer until I throw this bag of gold to you. You bow to me very low, *very* low and back out. Understand?"

Imogen was wearing an orange pullover and a light green skirt. I could see the gold band under the sparkling engagement ring.

"My God! The boy's not been listening! Now see here, young Olly—"

"Very difficult, coming in like this," said Mr. De Tracy softly from behind me. "I expect he's a bit diffident. I know I should be."

"Did you hear all I said?"

"Yes, Mr. Claymore."

"Norman, I think, don't you? He ought to know where to enter. It would be a help, wouldn't it?"

"He'll come in where that oaf Smith came in, of course."

Mr. De Tracy's voice was beautifully clear and gentle and he used it slowly, drop by drop, as if he knew how precious it was.

"Perhaps—*perhaps* he doesn't know that Smith entered through here, up stage, centre."

Mr. Claymore laid a fist on his forehead and shut his eyes.

"He wasn't in front last night, then!"

My mother spoke from the hall.

"He came back from Oxford very late. It was his Don Rag you know! They were very pleased with him, weren't they, Oliver?"

Mr. Claymore placed his fist on the table and opened his eyes.

"I was assured he would be in front, to get the *feel* of the thing!"

Mr. De Tracy vibrated and was still.

"We must do the best we can, Norman, old man."

"Righty ho. Now then, young Oliver. You start playing when I say, 'I'm beginning to find it the most enchanting place in the world.' Understand?"

"Yes, Mr. Claymore."

"And when I say, 'The music tells you what I cannot—what I dare not tell you!' Then you cut right down."

"Yes, Mr. Claymore."

I went and stood behind a canvas flat. There was eighteen inches between it and the cloth hung up as a cyclorama. Imogen spoke with her lovely voice.

"It is a strange, a haunted place. It frightens me!"

"I'm beginning to find it the most enchanting—no, hold it. I'm beginning to find it the most *enchanting* place in the world!"

I walked on to the platform and began to play, but stopped soon, because Mr. Claymore had stood up and was waving his arms.

"Stop! Stop! Stop!"

Mr. De Tracy had his arm round my shoulders and was patting my right elbow.

"Norman old man. I think you should leave this to me.

Solely to conserve your voice and your strength for tonight. Um?"

Mr. Claymore collapsed in the chair and laughed sarcastically.

"If you say so, Evelyn!"

He drummed with his fingers on the table until Imogen laid her hand over his and looked at him understandingly. But Mr. De Tracy was dropping his clear, gentle words in my ear.

"You play so beautifully, dear boy, that we must get this exactly right. Mustn't we? Um? Now *if* you come in with those splendid strides, you'll be right down here, within six inches of the orchestra pit before you've played a note to the king and the princess who are back *there*. On the other hand, if you only take one splendid stride"—and all the time his hand patted gently—"you won't look like a properly servile, obsequious, deferential gipsy musician, now will you? Um?"

"No, sir."

"Call me Evelyn, dear boy. Everybody does. And I shall call you Oliver. Um? Now let's just practise the entrance once or twice—yes. You see you must take a lot of *little* steps, almost putting your feet down in the same place; and that will make the stage look bigger, to the audience—believe it or not. Splendid!"

By now I was crouched so low I had a good view of Mr. De Tracy's knees and marvelled at the way the joints could move sideways so freely and quickly.

"Oliver, dear boy, don't tell me! You've acted before! Um?"

"No I haven't. Honestly."

"Not at school, even?"

"They tried me, but I break things."

"Madam, I congratulate you on your son."

My mother laughed invisibly from the hall.

"Oh Mr. De Tracy! I'm sure—"

"A natural talent, in addition to his *splendid* playing—Now. Are we all ready?"

Mr. Claymore laughed sarcastically again.

"We've been ready for some time!"

"Right, Oliver, dear boy."

" 'I'm beginning to find it the most enchanting place in the world!' "

I entered with tiny steps and played, waiting for the cue to go pianissimo but it did not come. Instead, Mr. Claymore stood up again and began to wave his arms about. I stopped.

"But it's impossible! Quite impossible! Oh, my God!"

"I was waiting for you to say—"

"But I said it! I *shouted* it!"

This time, Mr. De Tracy had his arm round Mr. Claymore's shoulder.

"Norman, old man, I'm going to *bully* you. And you can take it, can't you?"

"My God, My God!"

"It's temperament, you see. Calm down, old man. Better?"

"My God—"

There was a long silence while Mr. De Tracy patted. Mr. Claymore took his fist from his forehead and opened his eyes. Imogen gave him her wonderful, crinkly smile. Mr. Claymore dropped his head towards Mr. De Tracy's shoulder, gripped his left biceps and squeezed hard.

"Sorry, Evelyn, old man."

"That's all right, Norman, old man. I wonder. Should we break?"

"No, no."

"You're sure you wouldn't—"

"No."

Mr. Claymore flung back his head, smoothed back his hair and processed to his seat.

Once more, Imogen put her hand over his. Mr. De Tracy turned smiling to me.

"Somehow or other, laddy, we must—scale down. We must—how shall I say?"

He put one hand to his chin, and the spots on his yellow billiard balls stared into the darkness of the hall.

"We must—" He took his hand away from his chin and holding it out in the air, rotated it in a half circle, all the time holding something invisible between his finger and thumb—"turn down the volume!"

The gnat voice sang from the table.

"His father has a whatd'youmecallit on his fiddle."

Mr. De Tracy spread his arms wide.

"What was I thinking of? A mute! The very thing!"

"Oh no indeed," cried my mother from the darkness. "Oliver couldn't *possibly* use a mute! Why, I never heard such foolishness in my life!"

"Look, Mother—"

"Gently, Norman, gently. Let me handle this. You save your strength for the performance. Now Madam—" and Mr. De Tracy smiled moonily down the hall, his face on one side, "—pray why should your son not use a mute?"

My mother's voice came tartly up at us.

"Because he'll be up there, and everybody will see it!"

"It's a point, Norman, old man."

"They won't notice, Evelyn, old man, they'd be looking at the king and the princess. He's entirely incidental."

"Of *course* they'll be looking at Oliver, Mr. Claymore! And listening to him! I must say, if you can't speak loudly enough to be heard above a single violin played at the very *back* of the stage—"

"A single violin," sang Mr. Claymore. "The boy sounds like a brass band!"

"He's kindly consented to play for you and I will *not* have him—"

"Gently, Norman, old man. Sit down. You too, Imogen, dearest lady. Madam—"

"There's far too little consideration shown to the musicians in this production!"

Mr. Claymore struck his forehead then slumped on the table.

"I'm so tired. God. So tired."

We were all silent. Looking down, embarrassed, I saw how widely and rapidly Mr. De Tracy's knees were opening and shutting and wondered if he was about to fall. I spoke a bit sheepishly and hesitantly.

"I was thinking—there's—a trick—"

Mr. De Tracy continued to smile, mouth slightly open, spot balls looking deeply down into my eyes.

"Yes, laddy? Oliver?"

"It's just a trick, you see. Only—if I use a penny. An old one's best. Yes, this'll do. Between the bridge and the tail. You see if I—I'll have to let the strings down a bit. Then if I—like this. Wedge the penny over the A string, then under the D and over the G again—There. Like that. Then tune again, of course. It won't affect the E string much, but I don't use it much in this—stuff. There. Wait a moment while I get tuned up."

"They won't see it, Mr. Claymore. I hope you're satisfied. Now nobody will hear Oliver at all."

Mr. De Tracy gazed at me reverently.

"Genius. Sheer genius."

"So tired. God."

"Evelyn, I *do* think Norman has had enough—"

"Imogen, dearest lady, sweet friend—the play's the thing. Norman, old man, I'm going to bully you again. Once more; and then—nice drinkies. Ready, Oliver, laddy?"

" 'I'm beginning to find it the *most* enchanting place in the world!' "

By turning my head sideways on the rest so that my ear was practically among the strings, I could just make out a thread of sound. My other ear could just hear Mr. Claymore. We were a couple of gnats. I began to get interested in the phenomenon of this ghostly playing, but before I had finished, Mr. Claymore plucked a small bag from his pocket and tossed it high into the air in my direction.

"You'll have to catch it, laddy," said Mr. De Tracy, his natural voice, gentle as it was, booming among the gnats. "And if you miss it you'll have to grovel."

"Yes sir. Was that all right?"

"Perfect. Exquisite."

"I couldn't hear him at all," cried my mother from the back of the hall. "Not one note!"

Mr. Claymore glared into the darkness.

"This is an intimate scene," he sang. "You'll be saying you can't hear *me* next!"

My mother laughed, gaily.

"Well to tell you the truth—"

"Evelyn, old man! An idea! We can *use* him! To dress the big scene—just before the Great Duet! You remember?"

"Of course, old man. But he can hardly be a gipsy, can he? Not at the palace!"

I stood silent, holding my bow and violin, while they settled my future.

"Cries out for it! After all there were at *least* a dozen pairs of courtiers, lords and ladies, in the original production—"

"It's an idea, old man, an undoubted idea."

"He could be a guard. Standing at attention, sword drawn. Salute and withdraw."

"Where would you have him?"

127

"Here? No—there! Or up stage, centre, in front of the french window?"

"I *think*—down stage, right. Stand there, would you, laddy?"

"Evelyn, old man, when I saw Ivor play this part he dismissed the court with a gesture like *that*. But with one guard, I'd better say something, hadn't I? What d'you think?"

"We'll come to that, Norman. There's a technical point, though. What will he wear?"

"He ought to be a guardsman," said my mother. "He'd look splendid in one of those helmets."

"He would indeed, madam; but alas! All five uniforms are required by the chorus; and they will be lined up on the stair with the ladies, waiting for the finale."

Mr. De Tracy spread his arms again, head on one side and smiled at each of us in turn. He shrugged very slightly.

"Nothing to be done."

I breathed again; but then I heard my mother hurrying up the hall to the green baize curtain.

"Surely Mr. De Tracy, we can find something!"

"Look, Mother—"

"Ah, madam, if only we *could*—"

Mr. Claymore struck his forehead lightly.

"An idea. A thought."

"Yes Norman, old man?"

"I happen to have—I showed you my notice for Essex?"

"You did, old man."

"It was the Barchester Pageant," said Imogen, with a touch of animation. "*A Thousand Years of History*. Norman looked wonderful!"

"Now you see! I could lend him that and we could make a beefeater of him!"

"I quite see doublet and hose would fit a beefeater. But there's the hat, old man. Remember the hat."

"I have the very thing, Mr. De Tracy! An old, black, wide-brimmed hat of mine!

"Look, Mother, I don't think I—"

"Just a moment, Oliver. I could put cracker paper round it this afternoon and a rosette."

"Perfect. Quite perfect!"

Mr. Claymore was drumming again.

"Should we clear this with Wardrobe?"

"There's the colour too, old man. Shouldn't a beefeater be black and red?"

Mr. Claymore laughed.

"After all, we're in Hungary, aren't we? You wouldn't expect a Hungarian bodyguard to be the same colour as an English beefeater!"

"You think of everything, Norman. Hold on, though. He'll have to have a halberd. Essex didn't carry a halberd, did he?"

"Of course not, Evelyn," sang Mr. Claymore. "You're pulling my leg! I had a sword, a horse and a whole troop of servants!"

Mr. De Tracy smiled moonily down at him.

" 'Seven of my servants with an obedient start—' "

"More than that. But it's a point. We haven't got a halberd."

I began to move unobtrusively, off stage.

"Well that's settled then. I'll just—"

"Hold on, young Olly. Henry Williams. He's the man. Yes. I'll speak to him on the way home. He'll run us up a halberd in no time."

"I *believe*," said my mother from the other side of the green baize, "I *believe* a beefeater has a rosette on his shoes too—"

"You'll have a picture, madam, I don't doubt."

"Oh yes!" said my mother, laughing excitedly. "There's one in Oliver's 'Children's Encyclopaedia'! "

"*Mother*! My God—"

"Right," sang Mr. Claymore. "You can pick up the costume from my house this afternoon, Oliver, and get the halberd from Henry as soon as he's finished it. Now we'd better get the scene settled."

I clambered down and put away my violin, my penny and my bow. I tried to give my mother a fierce and dirty look, but the hall was too dark. When I turned back, Mr. Claymore and Imogen were facing each other in the middle of the stage, heads lifted as though they were staring at each other over a wall. Mr. De Tracy was examining a broom. He held it out to me.

"Here's your halberd, laddy. Down stage, right. You'll be standing there for all the last scene except the finale."

"Evelyn, old man, I must say something! Give me a line, will you?"

"You wouldn't prefer to move your hand, the way Ivor did?"

"I have it, Evelyn. How's this? But stay, your Royal Highness, we are not alone——" He turned and flung out his hand in my face. "Leave us!"

"Magnificent, old man. A really theatrical touch. Ivor himself couldn't write a better line!"

"Then he'll have to salute, of course."

"I wonder how you salute with a halberd?"

"He'd better lower the point to the ground. Try it, young Olly. Careful, boy! My God! You might have hit me!"

"I think," said Mr. De Tracy, when his knees were still, "I *think* he'd better not lower the point because it would go more than half way across the stage. Perhaps—Allow me, Oliver, dear boy. Stand like *that*; and when the King comes up to you in that magnificent way and speaks, stand like *that* and do *this*. Right? Then you can turn and march off through *there* and we can all see those splendid strides of yours once more, can't we? Try it!"

130

"Leave us, my man!"

"Oh no, no, no!" cried my mother, laughing lightly. "He wouldn't say 'My man'. Not the king! Not to a beefeater!"

"What rank would you suggest, madam?"

"General, perhaps," said my mother, still laughing. "That would sound very well, wouldn't it?"

"I am not going to call a boy like that a general!"

"He *is* a bit young for it, old man. Oliver, laddy. What rank do you feel? Um?"

"I dunno. I wish—"

"I'll call him 'Sergeant'. Will that satisfy you, madam? Just let us know!"

"Pray don't consider me, Mr. Claymore! I'm concerned solely with the music. But since you ask me, I should think that 'Colonel' would be about right."

"Colonel! Ha! Colonel! *That* boy?"

"Careful, Norman, old man."

"Colonel!"

"How about 'Major', old man, um? D'you feel like a major, laddy?"

"Major would do very well, don't you think, Oliver, dear?"

Mr. Claymore took three steps down stage. His fists were clenched by his sides. He was white faced, sweating, and quivering all over.

"Madam," he sang. "You observed just now that you were concerned solely with the music. Pray confine yourself to it!"

My mother uttered a high, tinkling laugh.

"At least I can *read* music," she said, "and don't have to be taught it note by note!"

The silence was awesome. Mr. Claymore turned on his heel and walked slowly up stage left until he was in the corner, his nose six inches from the painted flat. I stood, miserably looking at my broom. Imogen still sat, still smiled a permanent, sybilline smile at some private mystery. The silence went on and on.

My mother went suddenly to the piano, banged the lid, slapped music together. Even in that dim light I could see she was shivering like Mr. Claymore.

"Come along, Oliver!"

"Where?"

"Home, of course. Where d'you think? The zoo?"

Mr. De Tracy stepped into the middle of the stage. He embraced us all, from my mother's shivering brooch, to Mr. Claymore's curly back hair, in a gesture and a smile of infinite understanding and affection. But before he could say anything, Mr. Claymore began to sing to the painted flat.

"Never again. No. Never again. Oh, I assure you, never again!"

My mother banged the lid down on the keyboard.

"And I assure *you*, Mr. Claymore—never again. No indeed! Come, Oliver!"

Mr. De Tracy shook his head, in smiling affection.

"Artistes—artistes to the bone! Um? Now come everybody—boys and girls—Imogen, sweet friend! Um? How often I've seen it happen—highly strung—just a tiff—um?"

My mother stood, gripping the music stand of the piano with both hands and looking sideways at the stage.

Mr. Claymore continued to sing.

"Never again. Oh never again, never—"

"Oh look, Mother—let's get it done with!"

"Imogen, dear lady—"

"I'm hungry, Norman. *Please,* dear!"

"Artistes to the bone—"

There was another long pause. My mother laughed suddenly, on a new, lower note, then was silent again, staring at the piano.

"Come on, Mother—he can call me—Charley's Aunt if he wants!"

Mr. De Tracy laughed reverberatingly, inviting us all to join in, with his arms and merry face.

"Now I'm going to *bully* you all again. Um? I insist! Who's the producer? Um? Madam? Oliver? Imogen, sweetest, dearest? Norman, you old trooper? You can't carry *everything* on those broad shoulders, you know!"

The pause was a little shorter. Then Mr. Claymore turned his face slightly from the flat, and spoke, strangled.

" 'Captain'. I'll call him 'Captain'. 'Leave us, Captain,' I'll say that."

Mr. De Tracy turned his yellow spot balls towards the hall and smiled into it.

"Um?"

"It's a matter of complete indifference to me, Mr. De Tracy. *I'm* confined to the music. You must settle it among yourselves. I shan't say another word."

Mr. Claymore spun on his heel, fists clenched, opened his mouth; then shut it again. He stood there, looking. Mr. De Tracy continued to smile, mellow and gentle.

"Right! Splendid! We are agreed! And now—drinkies! Norman? Oliver? Ladies?"

"Thank you, Mr. De Tracy; but I do not care to enter Those Places—"

I had begun to put the broom back by the door of the Mayor's Parlour, and was looking forward to a quiet glass of cider or shandy, when I heard my mother's voice go on, high and firm.

"—and neither does my son!"

That afternoon, I got my gipsy costume and my beefeater's doublet and hose from Mr. Claymore. I took them home and tried them on. They were both on the small side; for though

133

Mr. Claymore was about my height, I found the doublet very tight across the chest, while the waist was so loose my mother had to do some tucking before it was anywhere near a fit. As for the gipsy costume, it had been built round someone half as tall again as I was, and only about a quarter as thick. For this reason, a sort of purple satin waistcoat would hardly come farther round me than my armpits; and the only part of the costume that fitted was a red, stocking cap which could be enlarged to requirement. It was fringed with gilded glass beads which tinkled when I moved my head, and I thought, bitterly enough, would drown out both Mr. Claymore and my muted violin. But my mother said they were most becoming. After I had tried them out I went down to the garage to get my halberd. Henry was there, and he was in the office and wearing a suit.

"Hullo Henry! You got my halberd?"

Henry turned from the desk.

"Well now, Master Oliver. It's a Saturday afternoon you know. We aren't all gentlemen of leisure, are we?"

"Oh."

"We'll see. One moment, now."

He chose a key from the key board, climbed off the high stool and went across the concrete forecourt. Inside the main building he opened a wooden door to an inner shed. My halberd was lying on a bench, supported by two wooden chocks.

"Oh *dyma vi*! That's a wicked looking instrument, that is! Whatever are you using that for?"

"I'm saluting Mr. Claymore with it."

Henry said nothing, and we stood side by side looking at the halberd. The blade was made of sheet iron, painted silver. Below it was a cluster of tassels; and below that again the wooden shaft was painted red. I reached out my hand.

"Careful my goodness! It'll be wet, won't it? What time is the performance? Half past seven I expect."

"What am I going to do? You won't still be open will you?"

"Only for petrol. We'll have to leave it somewhere you can get at it. You take that chock and I'll take this—"

With great care we manoeuvred the halberd out of the building and processed with it to the open shed that contained nothing but Miss Dawlish's little two seater. We laid it on the concrete by the wall.

"Now," said Henry. "You leave that till the last minute, Master Oliver."

"I shan't need it till about ten. Half past nine, anyway. It's for the last scene you see."

"It might be dry. I'm not promising anything, mind. But it might be dry. Is that paint on your trousers?"

"No. I don't think so."

"My goodness. That's what they call Oxford Trousers isn't it?"

"Bags."

"So you don't have to clean your shoes, whatever. Labour saving that's what that is. All right, Master Oliver. You fetch your 'alberd as late as you can."

"Thanks."

I hurried home and found my mother creating my hat. She was still in a state of suppressed but happy excitement. If anything, the row with Mr. Claymore had added to it.

"Come here, dear. Try this on."

I put the hat on my head and it sat on top like a pancake.

"You have your father's head," she said happily. "I shall have to take the band out."

"Where do I change, Mother?"

"Here, of course! Where do you suppose?"

"I thought—"

"We're very fortunate to live so close. Poor young Smith had such a *long* journey! And with his costume soaked, too! Wertwhistles have lent their waiting room for the ladies. Of course until last week they were going to use the Mayor's. Parlour. I do hope it doesn't rain again! It's such a pity we haven't a proper theatre!"

"Do I have to go out in the *street*?"

"Don't be silly, Oliver!"

"Dressed as a gipsy? And as a beefeater?"

"Now try this on again. Don't cram it down because I've taken out the band and you'll scratch yourself. Oh dear. No. I shall have to split it up the back. Have you time to get your hair cut?"

"No!"

"You're not being very helpful, are you, dear? That reminds me, I got you a splendid ruff from the butcher's. Mr. Danford was most kind."

"Not in the street!"

"I can't understand why you two men aren't more helpful. There's your father—well never mind that. Think of Mr. Harvey, coming all the way from Bumstead Episcopi with his double-bass behind that little car *and* with a sermon to preach tomorrow! For shame, Oliver! You ought to be— why, when Mr. Harvey was a young man he used to tow his double bass all that way behind his tricycle! I would hold my breath sometimes to see him come down the hill from the woods with his double bass catching him up. It was a relief to see him shoot over the Old Bridge, I can tell you! *Every time* there was any music in Stilbourne he'd come pedalling through the woods—though of course he *did* give up for a year or two after the load of hay fell on him. Old Sparrow was drunk and I always think it was *so* fortunate his boy tried straight away to get the load back with a pitchfork; and after he'd discovered the double bass, well naturally, he knew who was there."

"Look, Mother—"

"I'm afraid we shall have to split it further you know. I

hope it's all full of brains, dear! No. There are some people to whom things *just happen*! Rather like you, dear! Remember the time you fell in the piano? Of course he's getting old now, and to tell the truth, a little *deaf*. It's such a pity. On Thursday night he got the numbers mixed up on his music stand and played the wrong one. Fortunately they were both in three-four time—"

"They're all in three-four time. Always."

"—so it didn't matter so much because one '*Om*, pom, pom,' is very like another '*Om*, pom, pom,' isn't it? The only trouble was he played number seven instead of number four, and number seven is longer. So he went '*Om*, pom, pom,' on and on after everybody else had finished—for a whole verse in fact. The result as you can *imagine*, dear, was that the audience thought it was intentional so they didn't applaud. Mr. Claymore was *livid*."

"Yes. I can imagine."

"Now don't you pay any attention to Mr. Claymore, Oliver! Mr. De Tracy is producer. You do what he tells you."

"What part's he playing?"

"But he's not!"

"Why's he dressed like that, then?"

"He's a professional. From London. A term at Oxford hasn't made you entirely sophisticated, has it?"

"Finished?"

"Don't be impatient, dear."

"I'm *fed up*!"

"And don't be like Mr. Claymore, dear! Did you hear the very last thing he said?" And my mother lifted her nose in a Claymore gesture of the face so that her spectacles flashed—" 'Evelyn, old man, I shall spend the afternoon Lying Down!' But—" And she flashed her spectacles at me over my hat—"Mr. De Tracy can see further than most through a brick wall, you may depend on it! He has the measure of that man! He knows the only way to handle that man—any of that family indeed—is flattery. Did you notice how he laid it on?"

"Yes. I did."

"Of course we must seem the veriest amateurs to him. But he's always kind and cheerful—and *most* appreciative of the music. He told the reporter in my hearing that he thought the orchestra was worthy of special mention. He said he'd never heard anything like it. Though of course with Claymore at the helm we shall just get our usual 'The orchestra rendered yeoman service under the direction of—' I only hope they spell our name properly this time!"

"That seems about right, doesn't it?"

"I shall have to put a bit of elastic at the back here, so that the split doesn't open too wide. You don't want your hat falling off, dear! To tell you the truth, I'm *determined* that Mr. Claymore shall have absolutely nothing to complain of. He may quarrel if he wishes to, but I shan't take part! It takes two to make a quarrel, after all. Besides, we ought to let Mr. De Tracy take away a good impression!"

"His knees are funny, aren't they?"

"Knees? Oh! I see what you mean! When I was a girl, we used to call them 'Horseman's knees'. You were too young when Lord Cromer opened the Institute, of course. You wouldn't remember. I wonder if Mr. De Tracy was ever in the cavalry?"

"It's not very likely is it?"

"I'm sure he'd look most distinguished!"

My mother jumped up gaily, and tried on my hat herself, then handed it to me.

"It doesn't seem very safe at the back, Mother. It kind of rides up."

"Oh dear. You couldn't hold it on, I suppose? With one hand?"

"I've got to salute with a blo—"

"Oliver!"

"—oming great halberd!"

"I'll sew in a stay. You can wear it under your chin, like the sailor hat you used to have. I always thought you looked so sweet in it. There was HMS LION on the band. When we had that fortnight in Weymouth you went right up to some sailors and said, 'I'm a sailor too!' "

"Oh my God."

"Put the kettle on, would you, dear? We'll have a sort of High Tea; then if you're hungry after the performance you can forage when you come back. There'll be coffee and cakes afterwards, of course, but people don't really eat anything. Everyone's *much* too excited. That's right, dear! Now you'd better practise your violin."

"I don't need to."

"You don't want Mr. Claymore to have anything to complain of, now, do you?"

"Oh all right."

"And take the penny out!"

"Mr. Claymore—"

"I didn't mean for the actual performance, silly," said my mother, laughing again. "I mean for now. You oughtn't to have left the penny there, Oliver. It can't be good for your violin."

"I didn't."

"Leave it in the case!"

"I'll keep it in my pocket."

"So long as there *is* one. In your gipsy costume, I mean."

"I'd better go down to the garage and see if my halberd's dry."

"Don't be long, will you?"

I went back to my halberd, bent down and touched it. The paint was still tacky and I left it where it was. Henry, being Henry, was still in the office. But when I went to him and explained, he had nothing to suggest. This surprised me a little for I had grown accustomed to thinking of Henry as a man who settled things. I strolled home slowly, to find my mother ready with my tea and a newly stayed hat. My father was there too, gloomily munching his way through a Cornish pasty. My mother ate nothing but talked vivaciously and moved as though a foot above the earth.

I felt a great kinship with my father.

"Well, Father? Happy in your work?"

My father turned his head and looked at me solemnly. Then he turned back and went on eating.

"You might *answer* the boy, Father!"

"Bach," said my father. "Handel. What I enjoy is a *good grind*!"

"Some of the *King of Hearts* is very tuneful," said my mother. "You admitted as much!"

My father looked up with a haunted expression.

"Yes I did. That was the first time I heard it."

My mother supervised my change into a gipsy costume and advised me on makeup. My moustache was particularly fierce. Then they went off together to take up their positions in the orchestra pit. The streets near the Town Hall were a remarkable sight. Ladies in ample and most improbable crinolines, guardsmen with helmets and plumes, a yokel or two, flitted from one side of the Square to the other and clambered furtively into shelter up the stairs under the Town Hall. I was encouraged by this exhibition to think that I myself might not be noticed; so carrying my violin case I crept through the Square. But when I reached the stairs it was clearly no time to ascend them—they were jammed with helmets and crinolines. I thought I would investigate the chances of entering by the main door since any possible audience would surely not have arrived yet. I stole through the market space under the Town Hall and peeped round into the High Street and my heart fell first into my buckled shoes, then leapt right up into my throat.

There was a queue at the main door of the Town Hall. I had known, in some sort of abstract sense, that people would attend the performance; but here they were, solid, real and alive. I knew them all and by dint of a kind of interior determination and extreme care in my movements could pass them in the street without blushing too deeply or falling over my feet. Normally I hoped myself and sometimes believed myself to be at worst unnoticeable, at best, invisible. Now I saw that I was to exhibit myself, not in theory but in horrible fact to these real, queuing people; was to assault their ears with the inadequacy of my double stopping. My very arms began to shiver at the enormity of it and I shrank back into the shadows of the Town Hall and the temporary safety of its pillars. The queue filed silently into the entrance hall. From above my head I heard the sudden blast of Sergeant Major O'Donovan's trombone. It was the overture, and we were off. I hurried to the stairs but it was still jammed and I had another worry. I could not see where I was to leave my violin case; so I ran home again, thinking how calm and attractive our sitting room looked, and left it there. I ran back with my violin in one hand and bow in the other, and hearing that the overture was finished, began to burrow my way up the stairs. They were crowded with fierce and nervous persons who had no care for me nor my instrument. I managed to get up to the first corner, and was carried to the second by a surge of performers which left me only just off stage. It was here that I remembered I had not inserted my penny between the strings and I tried to get back down the stairs. This led to a series of passionate arguments all conducted in a whispering hiss and I lost them all. I could have cleared a way easily enough by brute strength, but some of the blockage consisted of relatively delicate girls and in any case I was carrying my violin. I pulled myself together and used my intelligence. Whenever a made-up face thrust itself into mine and hissed at me, I told it I needed a penny. Had it a penny? But there was not a single penny, apparently, in the whole mob, and some of them were even callous enough to laugh at me. Then my moustache fell off, and the crush was too complete for me to retrieve it. My last hope—that of being thoroughly disguised—was gone. I gave up, submitted to my fate and stood just behind a painted flat, waiting for Mr. Claymore to give me my cue. There was a horrible silent pressure coming now, not from the cast on the stairs but from the unseen audience. I began to shiver and my hands froze on the violin. Every instruction went completely out of my head.

"I'm beginning to find it *the* most enchanting place in the world!"

I took a splendid stride beyond the painted flat, and stood on the stage, blinded by the lights.

As I stood there, blinking in the light and frozen to my violin, there came first a solitary clap, then another, then a warm flow of applause. There was a kind of 'coo' in it. It was clear that I was recognized, known, the dispenser's son; clear too, that I was one of the right sort of people. In a flash I understood that the faces in the street had noticed me and had approved my conduct, or at least, condoned it. From fright, panic even, I soared to the other extreme of self-confidence. Upright, a musician to the fingertips, a violinist who had not merely got a certificate but could play as well, I struck my first chord. My fingers seemed warm and live, my bowing arm loose and agile. I had no doubts at all, and I played as loudly as Mrs. Underhill sang. When I finished my piece—knowing in advance that my last three spectacular double-stopped chords were going to be exact and stupendously resonant—the applause was instantaneous and over-

142

whelming. My new selfconfidence and selfpossession did not desert me. I was more accustomed to the lights now and I could see my mother at the piano, nodding her head and laughing and applauding. I bowed with much composure; and as I straightened up, a bag of money flashed past my face and struck the cyclorama. I bowed again, backing off stage. There was stamping from the audience.

" 'core! 'core!"

I had modesty enough to believe this was going too far. It was, after all, Mr. Claymore's scene and I did not want to spoil it for him. The sweat cooling on me, I edged myself back among the throng on the stairs, smiling gently and courteously to each person in turn from the height of my new stature. I had plenty of time, most of the evening indeed, before I needed to become a beefeater and already I was feeling it would be something of an anticlimax. Still there was consolation in the thought of how easy it would be. No playing, no acting. Just dress the scene. I came out at the bottom of the stairs and found the evening air astonishingly fresh. I stood there for a while, enjoying the sheer normality of things and the memory of my triumph.

Mr. De Tracy was leaning against one of the pillars a yard or two away. He was still smiling gently.

"Whither away, laddy?"

"I've got to get changed. Weren't you round in front then, sir?"

"I felt that standing out *here*—one was able to concentrate wholly on the music. Did you have any difficulties?"

"I didn't catch the money, come to think of it. And my moustache came off."

Mr. De Tracy smiled down and uttered sweet breath.

"Charming, charming!"

He felt in the skirts of his coat and produced a bottle which he held up to the light, discovered to be empty and replaced.

"I think the two of us might steal off for a drink, don't you, Oliver?"

"I'm in costume!"

"So am I. May I drop the ludicrous affectation of calling you 'laddy'?"

"Did you hear me play?"

"I did indeed. Something told me you didn't have a penny with you."

"I'm awfully sorry!"

Mr. De Tracy quivered about the knees.

"It won't have pleased your hated rival."

"My what?"

"Our splendid male lead."

I swallowed, looking up at him. He smiled back, breathing the memory of gin at me. I gaped, but strangely, did not blush.

"How—?"

"The manly feet turned ever so slightly in. The look of—hangdog adoration. Charming, charming!"

"I didn't—"

"Your secret is safe with me."

"She doesn't—"

He put a long arm round my shoulder. It was oddly pleasant and secure.

"She doesn't know much, does she? I think it's time you were cured."

"As long as I live—"

He massaged my shoulder.

"Shock treatment."

"I'm all right. Honestly."

"Ten guineas and a third class return. I suppose one can't complain. One does of course. And the need to escape is so desperate that by the end, most of the ten guineas—However. Come to the mausoleum."

"Where's that?"

I saw he was looking at the Crown; and broke out in nervous expostulation.

"Oh I say! I'd have to change, first! After all—I live here!"

"The only consolation I can offer you for such a fate, Oliver, is a large gin. You've lots of time before you dress Mr. Claymore's scene for him."

"I thought you called him 'Norman.' "

Mr. De Tracy nodded, gently.

"Yes, I do, don't I?"

"But oughtn't you to be round in front, sir?"

"I am," he breathed down at me. "You know I am, don't you, Oliver? You can vouch for me, can't you?"

I laughed excitedly.

"You bet!"

"And call me 'Evelyn.' "

"Like Norman?"

"*Not* like Norman, child. Like my friends."

"Golly."

Outside the Crown he held me back, and stood, looking at the Town Hall, his head cocked on one side.

"Judging by the complete absence of sound, Mr. Claymore is singing."

I giggled, loving him.

"Yes! Yes! My God!"

"I've produced them, you see—for my sins—so I know all about them. Particularly about *her*."

"How?"

"By what Mr. Shaw calls 'The woman in myself'. I have a great deal of woman in me, Oliver. So I know, you see."

"She's beautiful."

Mr. De Tracy smiled down; and each word was like a wasp's sting.

"She's a stupid, insensitive, vain woman. She has a neat

145

face and just enough sense to keep smiling. Why! You are three times as—Never let her know your calf-love. It would just go to feed her vanity. And insolent, the pair of them! Not ten guineas' worth, a hundred, a thousand—"

I opened my mouth but could find no words to say. Mr. De Tracy dropped his arm from my shoulder and straightened up, briskly.

"Well—Here we are."

He pushed open the swing door and inspected the entrance hall.

"If you bring over that chair for me, Oliver, and sit down *there*, we shall be comfy between the fireplace and the potted palm."

He disappeared through the door of the saloon bar. To alter the layout of this impressive building was an intimidating thing; but with a sudden sense of change I fetched the chair obediently. Mr. De Tracy returned, carrying two goblets filled with clear liquid.

"Perfectly executed. Your mother would be— No. That was unkind of me. I'm sorry, Oliver, but you see I have—" And he peered about in the air as if he might find the right word written up somewhere. "—I have—*excruciated*." He handed me one of the goblets and folded himself into the armchair. "One can't even say it's in the cause of art. It's in the cause of ten guineas and you are the first, literally the *first* human being connected with this outrageous exercise in bucolic ineptitude—well. Always excepting your lady mother of course."

"She's full of your praises."

"Is she, now? That's very gratifying. What about your father?"

"He doesn't say much, ever."

"He is the—vast gentleman in grey who plays the violin with a sort of a smouldering dexterity?"

146

"That's right."

"He uses the Stanislavski method. I've never *seen* a clearer projection of furious contempt. Not a word said. Eyes on his music. Every note in place. Smoulder, smoulder, smoulder. Why on earth?"

"Mother wants him to."

I tried my drink and choked.

"Take it slowly, Oliver. You'll find it very liberating. Dear me! I really *have* drunk a great deal."

"Liberating? What from?"

"Whatever you want to escape from. Be liberated from."

I was silent for a while, inspecting the close walls of my life. Suddenly I found a torrent of words in my throat.

"That's right. That's it exactly—Everything's—*wrong*. Everything. There's no truth and there's no honesty. My God! Life can't—I mean just out there, you have only to look up at the sky—but Stilbourne accepts it as a *roof*. As a— and the way we hide our bodies and the things we don't say, the things we daren't mention, the people we don't meet— and that *stuff* they call music—It's a lie! Don't they understand? It's a lie, a lie! It's—obscene!"

"Very famous. Made a lot of money."

I took a quick gulp.

"You know, Evelyn? When I was young I used to think it was *me*—and it was, of course, a bit—"

"Charming! Charming!"

"It's so mixed. D'you know? Only a few months ago I— had a girl on the hill up there. Practically in public. And *why not*? Was anyone in this, this—was anyone doing anything more—more—"

I broke off, feeling extraordinarily shaken as if at any moment I might burst into tears.

"Did anyone see you, Oliver?"

"My father."

Mr. De Tracy's knees opened and shut once or twice.

"You see, Evelyn. It's like chemistry. You can take it as a *thing*—or you can take it as a *thing*—"

"What is like chemistry?"

"Well. Life."

"It's an outrageous farce, Oliver, with an incompetent producer. This girl. Was she pretty?"

"Rather!"

Mr. De Tracy looked at me over his goblet, his two old spot balls very still, his mouth smiling gently beyond the brim, his lantern-jawed face moistened slightly.

"How enviable."

"You wouldn't have wanted her, Evelyn, with all those actresses and—she was just a country girl from Chandler's Close; though come to think of it, why on earth we——"

I stopped, trying to think what it was I wanted to say— something about Evie and Stilbourne and my father's bino- culars and the sky, something it would be easy to say to Evelyn since everything was easy to say to him. I peered at him and smiled affectionately. A slight mist had formed round him, leaving him very clear and lovable in the middle. I saw now why his pupils were spots. The irises round them had been invaded by the yellow of his eyeballs in flakes and crystals so that it was difficult to see where they began.

"Evelyn. I want the *truth* of things. But there's nowhere to find it."

Mr. De Tracy drew a long, shuddering breath and his smile increased.

"Truth, Oliver? Well—"

"Life ought to be—"

"Perceptive."

He inserted one hand in his breast pocket and drew out a small leather wallet. Still watching me, he took out a sheaf of photographs and held out the top one. The mist moved in until it was all I could see; or perhaps since I concentrated, frowning at the photograph, the mist was no more than inattention to anything else. Mr. De Tracy pressed the rest of the sheaf into my other hand, but I was riveted by the one I could see. It was unquestionably Mr. De Tracy. He was younger in the photograph, but his long nose and long chin seen in profile were unmistakable. So was his lean figure. The wig of dark hair he wore came down in a bob, half way between his ears and his shoulders, leaving visible a length of sinewy neck. His bare right arm stretched gracefully up away from him, the left behind and down, so that together they formed a diagonal. The ballerina's costume with its frilly white skirt fitted him closely and his lean legs led down, knees supporting each other, to pumps on his enormous feet. The feminine makeup made him seem even more masculine. I roared with laughter.

"What on earth's this?"

"Just making a point, Oliver. To the perceptive. Give it back, will you?"

But I was looking through the sheaf. The costume was the same in each and so was Mr. De Tracy. In some of the photographs he was supported by a thick, young man; and in each of these, they gazed deep into each other's eyes. I laughed until it hurt.

"Give them back, now, Oliver."

"What *was* it?"

"Just a farce, that's all. Give them back, please."

"I don't think I've ever seen—"

"Oliver. Give them back. And run along."

"Let's have another—"

"Don't forget you're going to be a beefeater."

"Oh damn that!"

"Nevertheless."

I looked out and was surprised to see how Mr. De Tracy

had moved away, yards away, though he was still sitting in the same place.

"I suppose—"

"We mustn't disappoint your mum."

All at once I remembered.

"You were going to tell me something, Evelyn. What was it?"

"It escapes me, I'm afraid."

"It was about truth—and honesty."

"I haven't the least idea."

"I was telling you about this place—about everything."

"I think it's time you went and changed."

"Is it?"

"Run along, now."

"Oh, I remember!" I laughed again at the thought of it. "You were going to cure me!"

His face swam into focus.

"So I was, Oliver. A going away present. Well. *After* you have saluted and gone off stage, listen to the 'Great Duet.' "

"Yes? And?"

"That's all. Just listen."

"Right. I'll come back and tell you—"

"I shan't be here."

"What, are you going round in front?"

"I shall—escape."

Suddenly he was close, holding up his hand and tapping his wristwatch with his forefinger. I saw what the time was and hurried away in a sudden panic. I huddled on my beef-eater's costume, then padded away across the Square to the garage. My halberd was quite dry but very heavy. I carried it over my shoulder to the back stairs but the roof was too low to accept me like that. I lowered it to the charge therefore and went on up; but the cast was lining the stairs and in a few seconds what had started as an entry became a furious wrestling match with madeup faces mouthing silent curses at me over the red shaft of my weapon. There were half bare bosoms too and scarlet mouths and bright clothes and a tangle of limbs. However, I stuck to my halberd, urged on by a desire to get the thing over and go back to Evelyn. I got round the first corner; but when I got to the second the truth was inescapably plain. There was no way in which my halberd could be manoeuvred round it.

If anything, getting my halberd down the stairs took longer than getting it up. For every member of the cast, while willing to be urged a little nearer the magic square on which we were performing the *King of Hearts* was mercilessly determined not to be thrust one inch further away from it, towards the cold night air. I got down at last and stood outside the Town Hall, wondering what to do. I leaned my halberd against a pillar and ran to the Crown, but Evelyn was not where I had left him. I poked my head and hat through into the saloon bar.

"Have you seen Mr. De Tracy anywhere, Mrs. Miniver?"

"He's gone out."

"Will he be back?"

"He'd better. He still owes for his drinks. Theatricals! *I* know them."

"Where did he go?"

"One of the beer houses I shouldn't wonder."

"I must find him!"

"What d'you want him for, young Oliver? An old——"

"It's about the play. Something's gone wrong!"

"Oh I see. Well. Try the Running Horse where the stable lads go. And tell him I want the money for those drinks!"

"Right!"

"Because if he goes off on that last bus without paying——"

"Right!"

I fled down the High Street towards the Old Bridge. The

Running Horse was almost empty but Mr. De Tracy was in the snug. He was leaning on the corner bar with his back and one elbow on it. When I burst in, he took one look at me and then started to shake from the knees up.

"Evelyn! What shall I do?"

It was remarkable how he could keep that pale, smiling, unchanged face while everything below his waist was writhing and shivering.

"Evelyn! My halberd. Where the stairs joins the passage at the back. I can't get it up!"

The shaking enveloped him and tumbled the gentle words into the room.

"He couldn't get his halberd up the back passage. They'll never believe it."

"What shall I do?"

"You'll have to enter from in front, then, won't you?"

This brought on a paroxysm of shaking; and at the very top of him his tiny tuft of plastered-down hair suddenly broke loose and stood straight up, like a horn.

"But they'll see me!"

Evelyn did nothing but shake. His elbow slipped off the desk and he got it back on again. I ran out of the Running Horse, thudded up the High Street. I got my halberd from the pillar and went to the main entrance of the Town Hall. I managed to get my halberd through the doors into the dark auditorium without much noise, and stole along the lefthand side of the audience to the green baize beyond the piano. I lifted the bottom carefully, and sensibly, with the blade of my halberd then thrust the shaft after it. Almost immediately I encountered a slight resistance which ceased after a thump! so I crept headfirst under the baize, pushing my halberd in front of me. Inside the curtain there was a small light switched on, an upturned campchair, and a copy of the *King of Hearts* with a lot of blue pencil markings on it. I got my feet under me and knelt up. This side of the stage allowed a very narrow passage between the flats and the wall; and at the end of it was the locked door—or part of the locked door into the mayor's parlour. Looking that way I understood why the resistance to my halberd had never entirely ceased and why, after the first thump, it had seemed to acquire a feeble life of its own, jerking and shaking against my grip and my thrust. A young man lay at the other end of the dark passage, backed against the parlour door, his head and shoulders hard against it, both hands grasping the blade of my weapon an inch or two away from his chest. He was very unreasonable and when I tried to get the halberd away from him he wrestled with it again, mouthing at me.

"But," sang the gnat voice of Mr. Claymore, "stay, your Royal Highness. We are not alone!"

I was late after all and jerked the halberd away from the young man who most unfortunately let go of it at the same time. I was thankful not to fall backwards on to the stage and glad that only a few feet of halberd butt had inadvertently projected into the light. I turned round therefore between two flats, took a stride and drew myself up. I was facing Imogen and could not see Mr. Claymore anywhere. Looking round for him, I found him in front of me, but bent down as if he were inspecting the buckles on my shoes. Imogen flung out an arm and her eyes blazed at me.

"Leave us!"

I was so confounded by her anger, and cowed by the gesture that I slunk away off stage, my ears burning. I did not even hear what the audience were doing. I stood my halberd against the wall behind the cyclorama cursing myself for having forgotten to salute.

The music began.

I found that my heart had not fallen as far as it normally would when I contemplated one of Imogen's perfections. It was as if Evelyn stood by my side. It was as if he still held his hand on my shoulder. The sweat dried on me. She had walked indifferently into a country to which I had access, of which indeed, I was native. In that landscape where notes of music, and all sounds were visible, coloured things, she trod with ignorant, ungainly feet. It was not just that she could not sing. It was that she was indifferent to the fact that she could not sing; and yet had gone, consenting to this public exhibition. She was so out of tune that the line of the song that should have been spiky as a range of mountains was worn down like a line of chalk hills. I listened, with Evelyn's absent hand on my shoulder and through the sound of the Great Duet—gnat now allied to drone—I heard his voice.

A stupid, insensitive, vain woman.

They were two people whose ignorance and vanity made them suitable to, acceptable to no one but each other. It was a spyhole into them, and ugly balm to my soul. I listened; and I was free. I pushed my way against the tide down the stairs again and ran to find the man to whom I now owed so much. But he was not in the Running Horse or in any of the four other pubs on that side of the High Street. I came back towards the Town Hall, thinking that of course, he must be round in front, waiting for the final curtain.

But I was wrong for he was in the Square. I saw him from a long way away because he was almost under one of the sodium lights. He was holding the sharp points of the iron railing with both hands and hanging down from them. His spidery legs were folded, therefore; and as if the life of vibration and quiver was in them only, they still moved. His face, in profile against the railings, had not changed, was still pale, still wore its gentle smile. His legs were going for little tentative walks all by themselves, then coming back again as if they had realized they had left someone behind.

I had seen this particular phenomenon in the quad at

Oxford often enough to realize what had happened. Clearly he was not going to be present at the final curtain. There was only one thing to do.

"Come on, Evelyn!"

He neither recognized me nor noticed me. I got hold of him round the shoulders and lifted him up. All his energy now seemed concentrated in his hands and I had to prise them away from the spearheaded railings. I half led, half carried him down the High Street; and there was the Barchester bus, the last one, waiting emptily.

The conductor did not much like the look of us, costumed as we were.

" 'As 'e been sick?"

"He won't be sick," I said, laughing, "not Mr. De Tracy —will you, Evelyn?"

Evelyn made no reply. I got him inside, for he was docile now, and weighed nothing. I sat him carefully and affectionately on the long seat just inside the door.

"There you are!"

As if he were some object suspended in water; or as if this was some action habitual to him and now inevitable, Evelyn moved both hands to his right cheek, drew his knees up towards his chin, and at the same time rotated to the right through ninety degrees. He lay there, curled close, his face, his smile, his spot balls quite unchanged, as if this way of looking at the world was as good as any other; and when the engine started, its movement made his body shudder as if this unusual view of Stilbourne was only the last in a whole series of private entertainments.

The conductor was doubtful.

"I don't know as 'ow—"

"He'll be all right. By the time he gets to Barchester—"

But it occurred to me as the conductor rang his bell that I had only assumed and did not know for certain that he wanted

to go to Barchester. I ran after the bus, therefore, shouting:
"Evelyn! Hey! Evelyn! You're going to Barchester—"

But the bus beat me, humping itself over the Old Bridge, and grinding up the road towards the woods. I turned back, wondering whether I should go home, get money and take it to Mrs. Miniver. However, the sight of lights going out in the Running Horse decided me that she would have to wait till next day; and if the money was an impoverishment to me, I could always get it back when I saw Evelyn again, or when he wrote to me. I went to the stairs at the back of the Town Hall therefore and found them deserted. I climbed them, to find the stage empty too, though a subdued sound of voices came from beyond the curtain. I applied my eye to a convenient hole and saw how the cast, stage hands, musicians and friends stood about, drinking coffee. They were in several groups that did not seem to have much interconnection; and I realized with relief that the SOS could not function again for at least three years. I opened the curtains and stepped down to receive my congratulations.

Stilbourne it said; but not as I had ever seen the name before. "Stilbourne" used to be traced in cracked and fading black on the signposts, which always leaned and sometimes pointed wholly in the wrong direction. Shrubby trees, elder, blackthorn or maple hid them, so that they only yielded their unneeded information to hedgers and ditchers. They decayed, waiting in the lanes for the stage coaches that would never come.

This STILBOURNE could be read at a distance of half-a-mile. It stood by the motor road, white letters on blue; and I saw immediately that Stilbourne was like anywhere else after all. Satellites must scan or photograph it, in their mathematical progress from Omnium to Barchester, a small huddle of houses by a minimal river—a place surprised by the motor road, as a ploughman and his horses might be by a helicopter. My hands turned the wheel of themselves, and without conscious intention I found myself gliding down the spur to all those years of my life. Sure enough, there was the Old Bridge, humpbacked and grey and uneconomic like so much beauty. No one had widened it or smoothed out the hump—and swinglike I lifted over it, then stopped my car with the curved ascent to the little Square before me. I examined my heart for emotion but found none. The determination never to return, lest I should find my heart wrung or broken by dead things, this I found replaced by a no more than mild curiosity. I was wary perhaps, and willing to run away, if nostalgia became so sharp, so raw as to be unbearable, but the glass windows of my car made a picture postcard of the place. I could roll through it, detached, defended by steel, rubber, leather, glass.

Yet not all the High Street was the same. The right hand side, almost from the Old Bridge to the Square had been swallowed by concrete, plateglass, chrome. It was Henry, of course. The lettering stretched up the street, Williams's Garage, Williams's Showrooms, Williams's Farm Machinery; and there, on the park which now lapped against the river, were examples of those objects by which Henry had changed us, haybalers and combines, tractors, hedgecutters in vivid orange or blue so that it was obvious how he prospered. Huge concrete pipes lay by the river, presently to swallow it, so that Henry would then face about and front on the motor road. I moved forward and pulled on the concrete apron by the pumps; and what Mark and Sophy have elected to call a "Petrol Lady" came towards me. She was plump and blonde, wore a white overall with "Williams's Garage" embroidered over the left breast.

"Is Mr. Williams about?"

She replied that young Mr. Williams was up in London but that old Mr. Williams might be in the office. So I got out of my car; and immediately my feet touched the concrete, I felt them become adolescent, with nowhere to go or hide.

158

I recognized immediately that this visit was a mistake; but before I could return to the security of leather and steel and glass, I heard his voice behind me.

"Master Oliver!"

He held my hand warmly, firmly, and for a long time; not shaking it, but moving it gently up and down, as if we were communing on the sadness of things in general. I had time to notice how little his thin face had changed—tanned, perhaps, by winter Egypt or Marrakesh—so sad it was, round the sad brown eyes that seemed always on the point of over-flowing. Only his hair was different. It was snow-white.

"My dear Henry. You go from strength to strength."

"We do what we can."

"And the cars you're selling! Nothing but the best."

"Well now, Sir, if you'd like to change?"

But he had seen my car, past my shoulder. He let go my hand.

"Well, now then!"

There it was, confirming what was always indefinably audible in the run and juggle of his syllables, the almost parody Welshness of him, like a runnel clucking on the side of a mountain.

"I can see why not, with a car of that superior description —*well* now!"

My feet grew up a little. It was the first time in my life I was ever conscious of impressing Henry. His attitude was typical of the deep thing lying in him, the reason for it all, tarmac, glass, concrete, machinery, the thrust not liked or enjoyed but recognized as inevitable, the god without mercy. There was a tiny adjustment in his attitude. He was deferring to achievement without knowing precisely what it was; and I, my feet now firmly under control, was accepting this deference. I went with him to be shown round, contemptuous of the way in which our social antennae had vibrated;

and it was only in the oldest part of the building, that I stopped before something that felt familiar even before I had worked out why. Here there were palms now, and potplants and soft lights, and among them, a turntable. On the turntable, brass radiator gleaming, coach lamps gleaming, old fuddy-duddy wheels newly tyred, hood folded back, was a vintage two-seater. It revolved with a crazy dignity like a dowager, presenting me now the offside, and now the radiator with the number plate below it.

I cried out.

"Bounce!"

"She let us buy it when she knew she was not going to use it any more. You can imagine we did not feel we could quibble over the price."

"She's dead, then."

"Miss Dawlish passed on—oh nearly three years ago. She lies where she would have wished, within earshot of the organ. Dear, good lady!"

I had no more than half an ear for him. Nor was I examining the two-seater closely, though I seemed to. I was busy examining myself. These feelings, these emotions that seemed suddenly to expand in a luxury more suitable to the palms, the potplants—

"She lies on the south side of the church, near the transept. We felt some tribute, some—memorial was appropriate. You can't miss it."

"So Bounce is dead!"

"You were always devoted to her, weren't you? I remember, indeed! You'll want to pay your respects."

I turned away from her car and looked at Henry. His eyes, as ever, were impenetrable in their frankness. You could never see round or through Henry. I felt myself, of all things, begin to blush as if I were a child again. I felt the power of his adult command.

"Yes," I mumbled. "Of course. Yes."

I took my obedient feet away from him and marched up the curved High Street to the Square. There was much new paint. They had washed the pillars of the Town Hall and painted the balcony glossy white. The grass in the centre of the Square, between the Town Hall and the church, was being cut noisily by one of Henry's machines so that half was disciplined, and the other half a diminishing oblong of mutinous daisies. The old chainrails round the grass had gone for scrap, and the posts with them. The old railings in front of each house had gone, too, but left their stumps in the stone. The familiar houses, bulged, leaned or slumped slightly out of true, had turned all Chelsea, with eggshell blue and one door of vivid yellow. I thought, critically, but without much feeling, that Stilbourne had been prettied, like some senile old lady, made presentable for visitors. Between the grass and the houses, the glittering cars were parked with their bonnets at the verge, like cows at a drinking trough. My father's cottage leaned against the doctor's house, not like a place for living, but as a visible piece of country quaintness, photogenic and sterile. The chintz which flapped lazily in my bedroom window had nothing to do with me. Only the church remained the same, in its stark greyness. Someone was practising the organ; and this sound, combined with the chatter of Henry's machine, reminded me of what I had come to see. I opened the lych gate and walked over the clipped grass between grey tombstones. I found Henry's tribute easily, since it was white marble, no expense spared.

The first impression it gave, was one of sheer weight. There was a rectangular surround filled with white chips, and among the chips, a glass container of *immortelles*. At the head, was at least a ton of marble rhomboid; and, finest touch of all,

F 161

this rhomboid had been carved with such a naturalistic representation of a harp, one might have thought the marble strings were vibrating in sympathy with the organ.

I looked round, wondering what I was supposed to do. One should know the appropriate formula. Was I supposed to be praying? How did one show respect? How do you show respect to clipped grass, chipped marble, the sound of an organ? The truth was, I was feeling glad to be alive and a little compunctuous at my gladness. I sat on a more modest tombstone, my legs apart, and stared at the inscription below the harp, as if concentration on her name would take the place of a more knowledgeable ritual.

CLARA   CECILIA   DAWLISH

1890   1960

Three score years and ten. Nothing either way. Expected expectancy. However I read the name and the date, they said nothing more, suggested nothing more. I lowered my eyes to the chips, examined carefully the *immortelles* which looked so inappropriately like part of a wedding cake. It was only when I examined the nearer surround—looked down, in fact, almost between my separated feet—that I grasped the true thoughtfulness of Henry's tribute. Here were three words in small lettering. They were placed there at the foot with exactly his modest assurance, his sense of position, of who was entitled to do what. Sitting on the lichened tombstone, with white marble before me, I fell into a kind of daze of remembering. They were not really Henry's words, nor Bounce's, though she used them often enough. They were her father's. Fishing back, grinning wryly, as I sat there in the sun, I could just remember him.

Old Mr. Dawlish. He was one of those eccentrics a child will accept as part of the landscape. We had a number of them in Stilbourne. There was one, a deformed halfwit in a wheel-chair for whom I felt no pity, since he was an object, like the horsetrough, or the illegible stone that lay against the town hall pillars. There was another, a strange lady wearing many skirts and a vast hat full of dead leaves so that she looked like an aged and emaciated Ophelia. Bounce's father, old Mr. Dawlish, did not look as eccentric as these two, certainly. But he was noteworthy. He was a failed musician, rumoured to compose; but in fact he kept a music shop and tuned pianos. By some inheritance from our town's complex interweaving, he owned not only the shop but also a house on the other side of the Square from my father's cottage. He had inherited a little money; and this, combined with his property, made him wholly estimable. He played the organ in church until Bounce was old enough to take over. But most of his time, while a bored girl minded the shop, he walked, or lunged, rather, through the lanes and streets. He was a slight man, in pepper and salt, and he had a shock of white hair which flew and tumbled above a fiercely aesthetic face. Always he looked up and to the side, as if preoccupied with some absolute before which people were shreds and tatters. Now and then, as he lunged through the streets, you could hear him—swept up, just like Beethoven in some tempest of the mind—cry, or rather, caw aloud:

"Aaa—ah!"

It may have been, that finding himself entirely without talent, he was resolved to give at least one first-class perform-ance out of THE LIVES OF THE MASTERS or turn himself into the portrait of a romantic musician from the brush of Delacroix. He believed, I came to know, in the New Woman, Wagner and Sterndale Bennett, though not in Mr. G. B. Shaw, or young Mr. Holst. Since he owned property, for all his eccentric lunges, he gave Stilbourne a painless excuse to feel that it was in touch with the arts as much as it ought to be.

I noticed him first when I was so small my nurse was pushing me up the High Street from the Old Bridge to the Square in a pushchair. I was interested because there was a Poor Man standing at the corner with a battered pram. He had what was much more exciting than a baby in it—a curling green horn which ended in a wide, trumpet mouth. He was turning a handle below the horn with one hand and holding his cap out with the other. As we drew near I heard a most delectable sound coming out of the horn—*Honkety tonk ti tonk ti tonk*! I laughed aloud and clamoured to be unstrapped so that I could join the children who were dancing round him. This was impossible, of course, since it was a public place, and the children were ragged and dirty. But before I had done more than give a preliminary whine, excitement piled on excitement. Mr. Dawlish came lunging across the Square from the church, a stick in his hand, his white, artistic hair flying. He made for the dancing group, and the Poor Man switched from my nurse to hold his cap out in this new direction. Mr. Dawlish, cawing like a furious rook, brought his stick down on the turntable of the phonograph, and pieces of black stuff flew all over the place. The dancing children shrieked and laughed and clapped and went on dancing. My pushchair slowed; then shot by, as my nurse hurried past the group, keeping well to the inside of the pavement. Naturally I was slewed in the straps of my chair, trying to enjoy the sight as long as possible; and in the few seconds left to me I saw the sleepy, sunny street fill with people: Moore from the Ironmonger's, Miss Dimble from the Needlework Shop, Mrs. Patrick from the Sweet Shop, three men from the Feathers, the smith with a smoking horseshoe at his halfdoor; these made a crowd in the middle of which white hair flew. There was no *honkety tonk* any more, but only rook-cawing, and the bird-dweedle of children.

Now you may wonder how, at the age of three, I knew these

people, their names and provenance; but a child's retina is such a perfect recording machine that given the impulse of interest or excitement it takes an indelible snapshot. I did not know their names or where they came from. But I saw them numberless times later and compared them with the snapshot that lay in my head, and indeed, still lies there. I take the snapshot from whatever drawer it lies in and sort my impressions into two piles—one of primary, ignorant perceptions; the other a gradual sophistication which tells me the horseshoe was cooling, my own white shoes made of kid, and Mr. Dawlish a thwarted man, violently acting out his prejudices and the drama of his fruitless ambitions.

I have early pictures of Bounce too. I was accustomed to the sight of this lady walking with her unusual clothes and elastic step along the other side of the Square towards the church. It was inevitable that I should learn some music from her.

I say "some", advisedly; for my father had a deep conviction that the profession of music was a perilous one and that I should descend through a course of indescribable bohemianism, to end, perhaps, pushing round a phonograph and holding my cap out.

Apart from seeing Bounce, I met her first when I was six. I went with my mother across the Square to the house where she lived alone and taught alone, one hundred and fifty yards from her father's music shop. My mother dressed with care, gloves, hat, a coat that pushed up under her jawbones. She opened our front door and let me out, opened our iron gate and let me through. We crossed cobbles and she bent, unhooked a length of chain so that we might enter the square of grass, then hooked it on again. To my eyes, the unvisited grass seemed vast as a night-time prairie for it was late Autumn and the gas lamps round the Square gave no light in the central area. On the further side of the grass, she unhooked another length of chain, then fastened it behind us. We crossed more cobbles, opened the iron gate of Bounce's house, and my mother rang a jangly bell by the front door. My left hand held a quarter-size violin in a velvet-lined case, and I was looking down at this when the door opened. I saw little but Bounce's feet at first, for I was shy, and I saw little more when we went inside for the house was dark. Her shoes were unremarkable, though heavy, and I watched them for a while, as the adult chatter went on above my head. As my eyes became accustomed to the qualified gloom of the entrance hall, I grew a little bolder, looked up slowly, and saw Bounce for the first time, close. I observed a severe grey skirt, the waist accentuated by a leather belt. Above this was a shirt striped black and white and narrow at the cuffs and collar. Down the front was a brown tie, fixed by a large brooch of some ugly, semi-precious stone in brown and black.

Halfway along the righthand side of the dark brown hall was a dark brown door with a dark brown settle beside it. After I had put my hat, my gloves, my muffler and my coat on the settle, we three went through the dark brown door into a darkness without any brown in it. All I could detect were two disparate eyes of faint light; one, a dull red spot low down, the other a blue bud, high up. Bounce's face approached the bud and turned it into an incandescence which illuminated the darkness without removing it. There was no pink or white in her face, only pale yellow, which combined with her high cheek bones, lashless eyes and hairless brows, gave her an appearance Chinese rather than European, indeterminate rather than female. At that time I thought of people as male or female by the nature of the clothes they wore, and the only thing definably female about Bounce was her skirt. Even her mousey hair, pulled back and pinned into a bun, was no positive evidence, since the bun was so flat as to be all but invisible from my level. But while I examined her mutely I heard the soft closing of the door behind me. I gazed at the glimmering bow window and heard my mother's step across the cobbles. When I looked back at Bounce I found she was doing something serious with a sort of rack that hung on the wall, so I started to examine the room instead. The darkness still crouched everywhere behind the hissing gaslight; but—as I was to discover through the years—even daylight could do no more than filter through curtains of yellowing muslin. Had there been no curtains, daylight could still only penetrate halfway down the room; for it was interrupted by an enormous grand piano that grinned savagely at the curtains as if it would gnaw them, given the chance. It had an attachment I have seen nowhere else—a complete set of organ pedals and the appropriate long, smooth seat. The lid was piled almost to the ceiling with tattered music, broken strings, a violin, books, dust, curious, unidentifiable objects, and the teetering bust of a bearded gentleman I later knew as Brahms. In the darkness beyond the piano was the red spot of the fire that smoked almost as much as Bounce. For while I had been examining the room she had selected and filled one of a dozen pipes. She sat at the organ seat and lighted the pipe; she drew, puffed, expelled long coils of smoke which joined an air already laden with dust and must. I looked away again at the rack, and then above the rack to the large, brown photograph of a lady in cap and gown, and the large, brown photograph of a man who stared bleakly across the room above my head. I looked back at Bounce, because she began to talk a little between puffs.

"There's—nothing—quite—as satisfying—as a pipe."

Immediately she had said this, she put the pipe back in the rack, and lit a cigarette. She took out my violin and bow and showed me what parts I must not touch with my greasy fingers. Then she began—the smoke making her eyes blink and run as she bent down—to put me into the correct position for playing the violin.

It is necessary to be cruel to musicians if they will not be cruel to themselves; and nothing is crueller than the position for playing the violin. That left arm bent, with its intractable elbow wrenched across the body, that wrist back where it must be to allow the little finger free play across all four strings—only the soaring voice from the instrument can justify it. If you found a skeleton twisted so, you would say it was a victim in the grip of a judo expert and just about to be thrown. Before we had any soaring voice either from her violin or mine, Bounce used my small body as a kind of lay figure, and arranged my joints with abrupt, manly, no nonsense jerks, pulls and pushes, a lay figure into which she inserted my still untuned instrument as an afterthought.

No sooner had I been fixed in a position for being thrown by the judo of music than I was unfixed, and my violin—that tiny thing which had glowed so when we bought it in the Bristol Arcade—was put in its coffin. Bounce put on a man's jacket and pinned on her flat hat while I struggled with my own wrappings. Then she led me back through all the bars and gates and chains to my father's cottage. The ladies agreed that I should be brave enough to go and come by myself in future. Bounce left me with instructions for my practice; a daily return to the judo position, left arm contorted, chin down, shoulder up, and subsequent insertion of my still voiceless instrument.

On Friday, ducking under chains, scampering across grass, I returned to the gloomy hall and knocked as instructed on the music room door. Bounce let out a large girl and let me in. This time, after some more judo, she tuned my instrument then made me saw away at the open strings. As a reward she took up her own violin and played me a scale, sometimes putting her fingers in the wrong places so that I laughed and made a face. Bounce looked down at me, severe as her skirt, till I became solemn. She made me imitate her exactly.

"Back, Oliver, back! Can't you tell when you're not in tune? You *must* listen!"

Sometimes she would grab and manipulate my fingers. Presently a tear ran down my cheek and dropped on the brown varnish of my violin.

"What's the matter? Aren't you well?"

She jerked away, stood two yards off. She lowered her voice to a whisper of distaste.

"You want to *go*, don't you?"

Yes, I wanted to go; but all I could do was nod dumbly. Bounce became very busy. She put my violin away quickly. She reached into shadows, took out a candlestick and lighted the candle at the gas.

"Come along."

I followed her; but she neither put my coat and muffler on me, nor showed me to the front door. Instead she went through the hall, then up dark, angled stairs, where the candlelight was no more than a puddle. We came to a long corridor and there were doors on either side, some open, to show a bare floor and a glimmering window. At the end of the corridor was a step up and a glass door. Bounce opened the door.

"There you are."

She handed me the candlestick and shut the door behind me. I advanced fearfully and saw a water closet of brown earthenware. Beside it was a handle and an iron rod which went straight up, miles up, through the ceiling. Behind me, I heard Bounce's manly shoes clump away down the corridor. I backed against the wall, and concentrated as hard as I could on the flame of the candle. I could understand now how I had mistaken her meaning and she, mine; but I was powerless to mend matters, and could only go along with them.

I stayed where I was against the wall and the ice of that darkness and remoteness formed on my skin and in my hair. The stump of candle shortened itself.

At last, far off, I heard her irritated shout.

"Oliver!"

I leapt at the handle and pulled it. For a few seconds nothing happened. Then, high up in the roof, there was a clank, a gurgle, a rushing descent. The unseen pipes hummed, roared at me, foamed. I burst through the door, tumbled down the step, and fled along the corridor. Bounce was in the hall, with a big boy who had just come in. She took the candle from me.

"That'll be all for today, Oliver. Practise that scale. I'll see you on Tuesday." Two yards away she bent towards me, as the big boy listened shamelessly. "And remember to *go* next time before you come."

So now I was fully launched on my career as an amateur musician. Tuesdays and Fridays, Fridays and Tuesdays. My mother was able to include my new status in her conversations with our few acquaintances.

"Oliver's getting on so well," she would say. "He's *devoted* to Miss Dawlish—aren't you, dear?"

I would agree shyly. There was not an admissible boy or girl in our society whose parents were not agreed on our devotion to Bounce. It was a rock in our lives, so real, so hard, so matter-of-fact. When I caught myself working out a sum; thirty minutes equals sixty times thirty equals one thousand eight hundred seconds, I recognized it as no more than evidence of my personal depravity. When I watched the clock, in the last hour before a lesson, I was very careful to 'go' before I went.

So now I knew Bounce and watched her across the Square

as she bounced along to the church or bounced back again. When she was not in the church, every half hour a boy or girl would enter the door beside the bow window of the music room. Indeed, she worked hard, did Bounce. This may have been the reason for a curious habit of hers which I discovered by accident and fostered afterwards as carefully as I could. If your mistakes were demonstrable, Bounce would correct them irritably. But if you could stay between what might be called the astonishingly wide limits of permissible error, her eyes would droop, her chin lift; and sitting on the organ seat of the piano, she would fall fast asleep. A cigarette would hang from her half-open mouth, and she would sway or rock or circle slowly like a top, until some loss of unconscious balance, or some crashing mistake on the part of her devoted pupil, would jerk her awake again. This was an incentive to accuracy perhaps, but alas, not enough incentive to cure my growing distaste for my tiny violin and the tedium of practising it. So I moved, as the months passed, through a series of crises, during which Bounce shamed me by contrasting my carefree life with the tribulations of her youth as a real musician. Once at least, she sent me home early in disgrace, since I had not written out a scale properly.

"I can't do anything with you," she said, severe as her skirt, "if you only work during lesson time. Now I'll tell you, Oliver. When I was a girl my father made me copy out fugues with a different coloured ink for each voice; and if I got a part wrong—Crack! went his ruler across my knuckles!"

So off I went, and tried to linger out my statutory half hour by following the man who was turning up the four gas lamps of the square with his long pole. As time went on, these glimpses of the Dawlish family life, fused into a sombre picture: Crack! over the knuckles with a ruler—Bonk! in the organ loft with a roll of music—Jab! in the ribs with the point of a bow—I came to a vivid awareness of lunging Mr.

Dawlish with his ready hand and his eye fixed on the absolute. Indeed, I sometimes wondered as I threaded the various iron obstacles between our house and hers if she might not call him in, when my shortcomings and misdeeds—my wickedness in fact—got beyond her own ability to cope. But fortunately this never happened.

The first break in my progress from lesson to lesson came when I took an examination in elementary violin playing. We took a whole series of examinations, because otherwise no one would ever know whether we could play or not. Once successful, we had bought—or our parents had bought for us—a certificate which could be framed and hung on the wall, or put away in a drawer as ammunition for the battle of life. But the examination was a turning point—seemed, now I look back, to have sparked off everything.

To begin with, it was the first time I ever rode in a car. This car I was to ride in was almost as big as a bus. It stood on the cobbles, alongside the iron railings that fronted Bounce's house, and we children gathered by it. Black winter had gone and there was sun; and we were excited and chattering. A man stood by the car; and though at the time I thought of him as just another grownup, I can rely on the retina of childhood again, take out and examine a snapshot. He was a lean young man, of medium height, with a thin, brown face, and eyes that swam as with glycerine. He wore a shiny blue suit; and he introduced me to the method of saying one thing with your face and another with your voice. He looked at a piece of paper in his hand. He said this was the house right enough but he's rung and rung; he had to see Miss Dawlish and he didn't suppose any of us were Miss Dawlish, whatever? His face was very sad and yet his words were a joke. Instantly he was a success. We all had our pictures of Bounce; and the incongruity of his sadness, our ourness and Bounce's bounceness nearly rolled us on our backs. But before exchanges could go any further there came an elastic step along the cobbles in front of the railings of the houses and Bounce was with us. The man put on a blue peaked cap, and touched it. Bounce took up a position two yards away from him, feet together, hands up a little, elbows back, and explained that she had been detained by the vicar. The young man opened a door and she ordered us in. After we were settled, she climbed unhandily into the seat by the driver, and we were off. There was no noise in the back of the car; and the two adults were silent in front; but a mile out of Stilbourne one little girl felt sick and attending to this emergency broke the ice. For as we rolled on between Dog Roses and Queen Anne's Lace we listened to an entrancing chatter from in front. The young man's voice had a liquid lilt in it, one most unusual in Stilbourne, a voice to match the mobility of his face. It varied quickly in pitch, was deft and light, like a musical instrument. Yes, he came from Wales, Cardiff, yes Miss, he sang a bit you know, was a tenor, he and the lads always used to sing a bit when they got together. It seems strange to me now that we learnt about him so quickly—learnt that he was poor, hard-working, eager to improve himself, a lover of music and a first class mechanic. We learnt from a strangely voluble Bounce what we had always known but never thought of, that there was no garage in Stilbourne, only the bicycle shop and the smithy; and that we had had to hire a car to get into Barchester because though we could return on the four o'clock bus, no bus went the other way until two in the afternoon, except on market days. The man wished he could read music proper, like you, Miss. He wished he could get into Barchester City Choir, which was about to render *St. Paul* in the cathedral; and forthwith he sang a phrase with passionate unction—"*Now we are ambassadors in the Name of Christ!*"

Bounce bent her head and looked sideways, smiling. She clapped her kid gloves together.

"Why, Mr.—"

"Henry, Miss."

"You have a very good light tenor!"

"Thank you Miss," said Henry. "That's a great compliment coming from a real musician like you. I'll tell them that in Barchester and then they'll *have* to let me in the choir. Indeed now, what would life be without music?"

"Music," said Bounce. "Ah—"

This "Ah—" was not one of Mr. Dawlish's rook caws but softer; and she added a sentence to it which sounded as if we were not in a car, but in church.

"My father always says, 'Heaven is music.' "

Henry nodded his peaked cap vigorously.

"You know the story about Dai Evans, Miss? When he went to 'eaven, it was a choir. There was fifty thousand sopranos, fifty thousand contraltos, fifty thousand basses, and only Dai Evans to sing tenor. They starts off with the 'alleluia chorus', and the conductor taps on the desk to stop them and says; 'One moment before we go on. Just a little less tenor, Dai, if you please!' "

This story affected Bounce much as Henry's first question had affected us. She shook, and cawed, and put up a kid glove to pat the hair at the back of her head. But when she was still again, I saw that Henry had begun to shake too, with suppressed coughs, tuss, tuss, tuss.

"I'm sorry, Miss," he said when he stopped coughing. "It's a touch of the old gas I expect. Now I tell you what Miss. It's my 'alf day. So you give me what it'll cost you in the bus— to pay for the petrol, like—and I'll run you back with the kiddies to Stilbourne when you've finished in Barchester."

This ended our silence in the back seat; for we all clamoured that she should accept. She did so, laughing, on our behalf and we rolled through the suburbs of Barchester to the hired room at the Golden Ball.

This first examination was to affect my relationship with Bounce for ever after. For when at last I played my ludicrous bit of Bach—da diddy *da*, da diddy *da*—I burst into tears of abject misery at the appalling sounds I made. Snivelling, then, I played a scale, putting my fingers on the shining places that would keep the notes in tune, however harsh. Yowling, I identified intervals with a kind of absent-minded certainty. Indeed, I told the examiner what note he played first, before he had sounded any interval at all, because I was so anxious to get the whole thing over.

"There's nothing to cry about," he said. "And by the way, I think you may have Absolute Pitch."

So out I went, sniffing; and by the time I had dried up, we were ready to embark again.

This time, Henry talked about cars.

"You ought to 'ave a little car of your own, Miss. The ladies quite often drive them now."

Absorbed as we were in the pleasures of travel—and I in my modest pride at being the only examinee to cause a commotion—it was only when we were over the Old Bridge and rolling up the High Street to the Square that I paid attention to what the young man was saying.

"Indeed, it's no trouble at all, Miss. I'll keep my eyes open and let you know when there's a bargain. And I could teach you to drive in a jiffy, Miss. It would be a pleasure, Miss."

We rolled to a stop by the railing in front of the bow window. Henry hurried round, tussing slightly, to let Bounce out. She looked us over.

"Millie. You have a long way to walk. You can come in and have a glass of milk and a biscuit. Mr.—"

"Henry, Miss."

"You've been most kind. You must have a cup of tea before you drive back to Barchester."

I hurried across the grass to my father's cottage, not looking back, so I cannot tell if Henry accepted or not. But when I told my parents I had been the only one to cry, they decided I was too highly strung for music examinations, even though I should not, therefore, obtain any certificates. I must, they decreed, learn music for my future pleasure, however eccentric this course might be; since it was clearly impossible for me to stop having music lessons altogether. The result was that a little of the strain went out of my visits to Bounce. She could not be expected to treat them seriously when they had no proper endpoint. She slept more often and longer. When she was not sleeping, she would talk, sometimes for as much as ten musicless minutes. I always nodded and agreed, for some reason. I could not disagree with her—*could* not. This obsequious agreement became a sort of straitwaistcoat.

Henry Williams reappeared while we were still in high summer. He turned up by the railings in a two seater with a tall fabric hood and took Bounce away in it. A week, and several driving lessons later, when I went with my violin—jumping the chains round the shaven grass, the evening sparrow's egg blue over the rosy roofs—the two seater stood on the cobbles with Henry beside it submissively. Mr. Dawlish lunged out of the front door, and tore open the iron gate, his white hair flying.

"A sheer waste of money!"

I stood there with my violin case, looking up. Mr. Dawlish turned, ten yards along the pavement, and shouted at the bow window as if it were a person.

"You've got your music haven't you?"

Bounce came out.

"Go inside, Oliver, and start playing."

Presently she came in after me, breathing heavily.

I should have to guess much more about Bounce and old Mr. Dawlish and Henry, were it not for the astonishing delicacy of my mother's perceptions. Like all the women in our Square she was a habitual detective. They, the women, were not satisfied with the railed-off enclosure before each house, nor with the spring-locked doors. They curtained the windows impenetrably. Standing back about a yard inside these curtains, they sent out what I should now call a kind of radar emission which was reflected from each other's business. A curious element appears in this; that to a certain extent the emission was capable of piercing a curtain, so that to a woman, each family was dimly visible, while each thought itself protected. The men had greater freedom, but clumsier, blunter perceptions. Nevertheless, they could bring back evidence of value to the trained intelligence inside. Each meal, therefore, was a kind of cross-examination which might allow a picture to be built up. My frail little mother, then, might stand behind our muslin curtains for half an hour, watching to find what a new hat, a meeting, a gesture, an expression even, could reveal.

"There goes the Eliott girl. She'll be going to meet young Thomas down at the bridge because her mother's still in hospital."

My mother had a secret weapon as well as radar. She had me. Not only did I penetrate Bounce's house twice a week, I was used over an even wider area. It was natural enough that I should help sometimes by taking bottles of medicine or packets of pills to one house or another. I never realized how deep my mother's interest was in whatever information could be extracted from me on my return. I was a kind of interplanetary probe, as ignorant of my mission as the machine itself must be. I remember in the days when Henry was teaching Bounce to drive, how I took a package to the house next to hers—Wertwhistle, Wertwhistle and Wertwhistle, Solicitors, whatever that might be. I went into a passage with nobody about; and while I was wondering where to go, a deep voice roared at me.

"Come in!"

I opened a door on a veiny-faced old gentleman who sat behind a table loaded with dusty papers.

"Well? What d'you want? Getting married? Making your will?"

I held out the packet.

"It's for my bloody son. No. I'll take it. Here."

He fished in his pocket and threw two pennies on the desk. However, I knew I was not a Poor Boy. I backed away, shaking my head, and shut the door. My mother was pleased with me for refusing the pennies and gave me a threepenny-bit for myself. Encouraged by this, I whispered that Mr. Wertwhistle had used a very bad word; and she nodded as if she knew he would, and why. Then there was a large house at the end of the side in which Bounce lived which had no other occupants than two ladies. There was a mystery about them that defied radar. When they had been dead for half a generation, I asked my mother about them but she would say very little.

"They behaved very strangely. Very strangely indeed."

I went to that house once. As if she had been waiting for me, the younger lady met me on the doorstep, pulling the door shut behind her.

"Tell your mother, Oliver," she said stonily, "that this is number seven, not number eleven."

I suppose that was game, set and match. And ruefully I remember how the Ewans always gave me a present at Christmas. They also vibrated in time to the crystal pyramid.

It is not surprising then, that my mother was interested in Bounce. I had described to her the angled stairs, the long corridor and empty rooms. At table she would sometimes embark on a monologue which was accompanied every now and then by my father's noncommittal grunts.

"Living by herself in that great house—"

Great house? This only confirmed what I had found recur in dreams—Bounce existing in a dark emptiness, a house empty of life except for the grinning piano. Mr. Dawlish himself lived over his shop, perhaps because he didn't like the house, or didn't like the sound of music lessons, or simply thought his daughter ought to be emancipated.

"She ought to let part of the house," said my mother. "I don't think a woman ought to live by herself like that. And the money—"

"Come now, Mother," said my father. "Dawlish has a considerable property. Very considerable. *He*'s all right."

Once, Henry arrived with the car while we were at table. My mother jumped up as soon as she heard the horn and peered through the curtains.

"Another lesson," she said. "That's the third this week."

My father wiped his grey moustache and bent ponderously over his soup again.

"That'll cost her a pretty penny."

"Nonsense," said my mother testily, "she's not paying him anything."

"Really?" said my father. "Well that's really kind. If everybody—"

"Kind?" cried my mother—with the sort of passionate contempt she kept for people not fitted with radar—"Kind? It's a sprat to catch a mackerel!"

Soon after this I saw the first time Bounce ever had the car to herself. It was one teatime. Bounce and Henry had returned to the house and then he had taken himself off to return to Barchester by bus. Bounce went indoors, leaving the car on the cobbles. We stood behind the curtains. Here and there round the Square, you could see how other people's curtains quivered, or were even drawn aside a little. Bounce came out again, got into the car, made motions with her arms and the car began to tremble. A dense cloud of smoke formed behind it and the noise of the engine lifted to a scream. The car jerked forward two yards and stopped dead. Bounce climbed out and went into the house; and next morning Henry was back, lying on the cobbles in his shiny blue suit, his peaked cap hanging on the radiator. But the next time I went for a lesson, I had to wait as much as ten times sixty, until Bounce rolled up on the cobbles, then bounced into the room, mannishly gruff and very excited.

"I've been right round the downs—oh almost as far as Devizes—by myself, Oliver! Think of that! It's quite easy really!"

She was making quick movements here and there, hands up. She exclaimed how kind Henry had been.

"And all in his own time! Do you know, Oliver, I can't get him to take a penny? He said it didn't cost him anything—"

I explained gravely, not only with a wish to agree, but also to use a new phrase that had delighted me, that he was "Using a sprat to catch a mackerel." Bounce stood very still, went very quiet. She began to cross-question me more and more fiercely until she was very angry indeed. I could not think what I had done wrong; and when at last she sent me off things were no better at home for my account of the meeting made my mother even more angry than Bounce. I never understood their two angers and it remained one of the unforeseeable perils of interplanetary travel.

It was at this time that I noticed something in Bounce's face that I was to watch intensify. I suppose an anatomist would define it as unusually powerful sphincter muscles round the mouth. If she was being severe, or condemning something, her mouth would contract so that her lips were first bunched then pulled in. For an inch around them lines would appear, all leading to the centre. Year by year these lines of the sphincter deepened until they were permanently visible whether she was angry or not. If she was angry, the lines deepened into corrugations, and her mouth was like an implosion.

No sooner had Bounce learned to drive than her father lunged finally out of our ken and was buried in the church-yard near the lych gate. I remember how soon after I had heard this I crossed the Square for a lesson and found Bounce's house deserted. I was nervous of the dark hall, so I let myself into the music room with its shadows and massive shapes and dim keyboard grin. The fire was smouldering redly and I went near it for company. A click from the dying coal made my hair prickle and if there had been any light in the hall I would have fled. But I stayed where I was and presently I could make out the shapes of things. In particular there was a shape on the mantelpiece over the fire in which the face became clear to me, bit by bit; and at last I could see that it was Beethoven, with floating, bronze hair, com-pressed lips, and deep eyes that bored furiously into the tail of the piano. He was so clearly of the same sort as Bounce and her father, that he seemed to accuse me. While I was meditating this the carriage lights of Bounce's car swept over the window. She came into the hall, paused, then opened the music room door. She went to light the gas and I moved forward in relief, knocking my violin case against the piano as I did so. She cried out, then whipped round—and there she was, staring at me under the gaslight out of eyes so wide there seemed to be no lids to them. She put one hand to her chest and sank on the organ seat.

"You must never, never come into the music room unless I call you in!"

I said I was sorry, humbly enough, and did not mind her anger much this time, what with the light and company; and presently we had our lesson. That same week, Henry Williams moved to Stilbourne. I cannot remember the exact occasion. It was merely the start of a new phase, in which we became aware of him as part of the scenery. At the top of the curved High Street, where it joined our Square by the Town Hall, was the smithy, separated from Bounce's house by a little lane. A few yards down the lane was a gateway which led into the yard behind the forge. At the back end of the yard was a sort of cowshed with a loft. Henry lived in the loft as if he were a pigeon. Sometimes he helped the blacksmith, sometimes he cleaned Dr. Ewans's car, or pumped up its tyres with a foot pump. When the market was held under the little Town Hall, Henry would be there among the stalls, helping generally, and generally available. Bounce parked her car in the yard; or rather Henry parked it there for her, since the lane was not ample enough for her manoeuvres. Henry serviced her car too, and cleaned it as if it were the crown jewels, so that it winked and shone. Half-consciously, I thought of Henry as belonging to Bounce because she treated him like that. She would stand in the yard between a heap of rusting iron and a tangle of nettles and talk loudly about the car as he cleaned it—talk gruffly from two yards away, but at the same time kindly, jovially, as if the car were a living thing and she was stroking it. Henry would work submissively and nod, until Bounce turned abruptly and bounced back to her house.

I could not understand my mother's pitying amusement. Why should not Miss Dawlish be devoted to her car? I should have been just as devoted in her place. But—and this was impossible to understand at all—my mother did not seem to like Henry. I on the other hand liked him very much and ultimately felt this to be another of my deficiencies. He would talk to me as I watched him, in his lilting voice, and he treated me with courteous respect. If he met me when he came to the dispensary for cough mixture, he always called me "Master Oliver", tussing slightly.

When the yard behind the smithy altered between one week and the next—acquired shiny tools, vats of oil and cans of petrol—and I described this new triumph of Henry's with excitement my mother cut me off.

"Pooh! I haven't any patience!"

Despite the death of her father, possession of a car seemed to make Bounce herself more amiable. She slept more soundly on the organ seat, her mouth lax and mobile as a baby's. She even evolved a joke which we were accustomed to share from lesson to lesson. I had a new set of violin exercises by some foreigner called Kummer. The coincidence of my late arrival one evening and the arrival of this green volume with KUMMER on the front did it.

"I shall call you 'Kummer'," she said, "because you don't come!"

She shook and cawed on the organ seat. After that, she would call me nothing else and we had many a good laugh together. When the vicar found us one day by the railing before the bow window, she got him to share our joke.

"I call him Kummer because—"

At the end of this term, however, she astonished me as much as she had ever done in her life. I was ten and had just begun at the local Grammar School. I carried a half-size violin now, which I played just as badly as the quarter-size one. I went to her front door, hearing from the yard Henry's click! clink! though the blacksmith had shut down for the night and gone over to the Feathers. I tapped at the music room door and Bounce was ready for me, because she spoke at once, though softly.

"Come in, Kummer!"

I went in, and found myself with my nose a yard from her shirt front. I was opposite one of the pearly buttons on the band or front facing, whatever it was, down the middle. This in itself was a change, for I was used to seeing the brown tie there. But there was more to come. On either side, between the band and the shirt proper, there was now a frill of white and scalloped muslin. Her hands were raised; and more scalloped muslin projected from inside each cuff. As my eye followed the decorated band up to her neck, I discovered that the brooch now lay in a nest of frills where the knot of her tie had been; so in my astonishment I looked up to her face. It had softened and brightened mysteriously—a face if not young, at least with a hint, a memory of youth, of girlhood. Even her hair had flowered out of its severity, was enlarged and cloudy. Her eyes—but it did not take them long to read the incredulity in mine. Her lips sucked in their surround of wrinkles, the hollows defined themselves beneath each cheek bone; and for the first and last time in my experience of them, a round, pink flush appeared on each. As I watched, this flush spread, over her face till she was dusky from forehead to throat. She went abruptly to the piano so that I could tune my violin, left me with a scale to play, then positively—her face turned away—rushed out of the room. When she came back, her face was its usual pale yellow and quite unqualified by frills. She was severe and very critical of my playing. I never saw the frills again.

For not long after this our whole situation altered. I was coming back from buying sweets in the High Street and stopped as usual to see if Henry was in his yard. This was always a matter of some anxiety for me since my mother did not approve of my pestering him. My time there had a feeling of forbidden fruit which as usual made it even more attractive. Sometimes, if he happened to be cleaning a car he would talk while I stood; and he would tell me for example what a sump was, or why tyres had patterns on them. But on this occasion Henry was not alone. There was a tall, blonde woman with him, a woman pale, adenoidal and gormless, who stood at the bottom of the ladder up to the loft with a baby in her arms. She was arguing with him.

"Well I'm not going to, see? It's no good, Henry. I got to have stairs!"

I went away with my sweets while Henry was replying liquidly. The blonde and the baby were Henry's quite unforeseen wife and child. I envied them very much, for it seemed a wonderful thing to me not to have a proper house but to camp in the loft like Gipsies. As for Bounce, I cannot tell down what chasms of humiliation and bitterness she was thrown or threw herself.

"Poor soul!" said my mother, laughing and shaking her head pityingly. "You'd never believe it, would you?"

"Believe what, Mother?"

But my mother went on laughing and shaking her head. This was a most exhilarating time for everyone; and I shared the exhilaration without understanding its source, perhaps on the unconscious principle that one should get any enjoyment that was going. But just when the exhilaration was lifted to a new height I found myself alone in the enjoyment of it. For only a few weeks after Mary Williams turned up with baby Jacky, they all three moved into the big house and shared it with Bounce. This made me particularly happy, gave me the peace of exorcism and I no longer dreamed of the long corridor and the empty rooms for I knew that Henry lived in them. Now, when I took a bottle of tonic across for Mary's anaemia, I did not turn right into the music room but left, down into the yard beside the kitchen and scullery with a glimpse of a long, unkempt garden; and there would be a pram on the flagstones with Jacky squealing in it and an invisible Mary clattering dishes. Yet my mother did not share my peace and happiness. She was unaccountably bitter when she spoke of Henry, and exasperated when she spoke of Bounce. I could not understand precisely how I was to adjust my attitude in this matter. When I was not in Bounce's presence I imitated my mother; and got an astonishing rebuke from Henry of all people. I took my bicycle into his yard one day to have the handlebars firmed up, and I spoke about Bounce as if he and I and all of us were on one side of a fence, and she on the other, with the Stilbourne eccentrics. He looked up at me out of a face smudged with oil, and with eyes swimming as ever in glycerine.

"Indeed," he said, "Miss Dawlish is a dear, kind lady."

So I stood, silent and blushing a little.

My father acquired a primitive wireless set and a little later, a gramophone. I began to understand what music might be, and what playing might be. Kreisler, Paderewski, Cortot, Casals—despite the hiss from the clumsy discs, despite the permanent frying crackle and bursts of morse from the headphones of the wireless set, music came through. But Bounce—when I tried to share this new happiness with her—attacked my father, attacked me, with a savage indignation.

"*Why* has your father done this, Oliver? He's supposed to *like* music! I would never, *never* listen to anything so cheap, nasty, vulgar, blasphemous——"

I stood, nodding and smiling, in a half-embarrassed, half-ingratiating way and hoped only that she would stop. There came a knock at the music room door; and after her exit I heard her shouting.

"I must *not* be interrupted, Mary, when I'm teaching! Very well. I'll have the steak and kidney warmed up."

Indeed, we were changing, all of us. Bounce was becoming more manly and abrupt, less elastic in stride, and a little fatter. With Henry and Mary she was rough, proprietary. Sometimes she would refer to them as 'My family'. Henry had changed too. He was solider. Instead of the shiny blue serge and peaked cap, he sometimes wore an overcoat and trilby, like the other business men of the town. As for me, I was becoming devious, secretive and cynical. It was a generation later that I discovered, on looking back, *why* I felt myself to be full of dishonesty and guilt. As for Mary Williams, she simply became more faded, more adenoidal; and sourer. Once, when I took over her bottle of tonic, and let myself into the yard, I saw Bounce standing on the flagstones and Mary Williams akimbo in the doorway of the scullery. They were both talking loudly at the same time; and then Mary raised her voice in a kind of whining scream that came through loud and clear.

"All I say is, Auntie Cis, I got to have my kitchen!"

Then they saw me, standing by the door from the hall, holding out the bottle. There was silence, except for Jacky, who threw a rattle out of his chair and made a loud remark.

"Bub! Bub!"

I delivered the tonic without a word said, and went away in the silence.

Once, when I sat in the dicky seat of her car—we were going over to Calne, to play and sing in the Elijah—Bounce and Henry were sitting in front. The hood was down and I halfheard a long, muttered conversation, which built up to the point where Henry cried out vehemently.

"No, Auntie Cis! It's not like that at all, at all!"

After more mutter, he spoke out clearly again.

"But then, like you always say, you got your music."

"—Kummer, there in the back—"

She slewed in her seat and shouted at me.

"Don't you think, Kummer?"

"What, Miss Dawlish?"

"Can't you hear what we're saying?"

"What d'you say, Miss Dawlish? I can't hear you. The wind makes so much noise—"

A devious child; but I had my music too. For I had discovered the emotional confirmations and enlargements of
music, not as a supposition, but as a fact of experience; and
though I still endured the violin I had fallen in love with the
piano and was bashing the last use out of our tinny upright.
I had heard more music than Bounce already and realized
the limitations of her musical world. It is worth considering
what those limitations were. Her great occasions were in-
accurate and not very lively performances of St. Paul, the
Messiah, the Elijah, some Stanford, and Stainer's Crucifixion
every Easter. For the rest, it was Heller, Kummer, Matthay's
Relaxation Exercises, with Hymns Ancient and Modern on
Sundays. As for me, I could only just bear—because it was
inevitable—the contrast between my ingratiating exterior and
the unvoiced thoughts and unanalysable feelings that flittered
behind it as twice a week I passed my useless half-hour.

"I don't know what Oliver would do, without Miss Dawlish. He's *so* devoted to her—"

And I would think, confusedly, next time I hid behind my
nods and smiles and listened to a diatribe about the Stravin-
sky she had never heard—

"*This is what devotion feels like.*"

She was broad now, her hair escaping sometimes from the
bun behind the flat hat. She had acquired two gold teeth on
one side that gleamed if she gave one of her no-nonsense
laughs, in man-to-man jolliness. The pram was occupied now
by Jacky's little sister.

"Come and look at my little niece. Ouji-ouji cluck, cluck!
This is Kummer, Di. I call him Kummer because—"

But one dreadful time, waiting for my lesson in the dark
hall I heard her voice from the stairs, not manly but earnest
and ludicrously pleading—

"All I want is for you to need me, need me!"

Indeed, my fading lessons on the violin were interrupted more and more frequently. It was not the rows that seemed to blow up daily in the old house, nor even the elaborate reconciliations. These did not interrupt my playing; they merely delayed it. The real trouble was the noise, sometimes rhythmically nagging, sometime suddenly shattering, that came from outside the house. It came from what had once been the yard and smithy next door, now turned as cheaply as possible into a workshop garage for Henry. Here were Dunlop advertisements, and old inner tubes hanging on the whitewashed walls like drying octopuses. Here were oil cans, oil drums, a compressor, a workbench and the few enigmatic instruments that were necessary to Henry's mechanical surgery. The whole place had the shine of oily dirt that comes with internal combustion.

I was, I remember, demonstrating my comparative ability to cope with the second position. Bounce was sitting on the long organ seat. Her square shoes were on the organ pedals, her tweed skirt and jacket hairy in the gaslight. As I played, her full chest swayed forward, her head dropped a little and her eyes closed. I was thankful and played carefully to her shut eyes and the unconscious sphincter movements of her mouth—

And then the noises were in the room like cannon shells. The shells burst all around me. Bounce was awake and glaring at my music as if the gunner had been part of the score.

"Henry," I shouted fatuously, "Henry working late!"

"So am I working late!"

She swung her feet off the pedals, jumped up and flung the door open.

"Mary! Mary!"

There was a pause, in which the noises went on.

"Mary! How am I to attend to my music with that hideous noise going on? He must stop it at once!"

I could hear Mary whine her answer, but not what she said. Bounce's voice, used to competing with choirs, came through strongly despite the cannonade.

"You must go and speak to him at once!" Then, *appassionata*—"I won't have it!" There was a brief, ragged duet in the hall which ended with two slammed doors as Mary whined back to bathing the baby and Bounce stamped on to the cobbles with a final fortissimo "I won't have it!"

I stood waiting, as numbers added up to sixty, to a hundred and twenty, to three hundred at last—and silent evening returned to Stilbourne. Six hundred seconds. Bounce came back, breathing heavily, her face shining, hair draggling from the bun. The cannon fire started again so that she had to shout the explanation.

"It's the Ewans's car. He has an emergency call and Henry's hired out his own. Mine's in dock. There's nothing to be done about it. You'll have to go, Kummer. I can't teach in a noise like this."

So off I went, pursued by cannon fire.

More and more Henry worked late. His noises were always unavoidable. Since most of Bounce's pupils had their lessons in the evening the collision was head on. I took my lessons in a house torn with quarrels, loud with mechanical noise, and hot with resentment. I began to notice how readily the lines on Bounce's forehead could turn into deep grooves. There was an utter exhaustion in her gruffness and her sleep on the organ seat. Then, between one lesson and the next, the noises stopped and Mary was all "Dear Auntie Cis!" again.

I learnt the reason at the tea table. My mother dropped a remark into our ruminative silence, which as usual, was a sign she had news for us.

"He's got what he wanted at last, then."

I looked up.

"Who?"

"Henry Williams. It makes me want to stamp my foot!"

My father looked over his cup.

"What's Henry Williams got?"

"Everything he wants. He's going to take over the shop her father left her—and the cottage next to it—and build a garage!"

I reflected on this for a while. No more cannon fire; and in consequence, a full thirty times sixty times sixty.

"Bounce'll be pleased, at any rate."

My mother clattered the teacups testily.

"You don't know what you're talking about. He's using her own money to re-build her own property. He'll have her last penny!"

My father peered at her through his pebble glasses and wiped his grey moustache with both hands.

"Young Williams works hard. She'll get her money back."

My mother laughed with a bitter irony, that strangely enough seemed to include my father with Henry.

"A likely story!"

"Now come, Mother. She's not a child. There must have been an agreement drawn up."

"Kiss me leg!" snapped my mother, using a childhood expression, the euphemistic nature of which always seemed to escape her, "Kiss me leg! You know old Wertwhistle's half-seas over all the time!"

"Well I don't know, Mother—"

My mother was remarkably angry.

"Well I *do*!"

We were cowed, both of us—he, perhaps, understanding her anger as she watched him plod back to the dispensary.

So now there was a new thing to watch in the High Street, halfway between our Square and the Old Bridge. There was a forecourt of concrete where old Mr. Dawlish had lived and lunged, there was a garage and a pit for inspecting the entrails of cars. There was a tall, thin structure next to the road, by means of which Henry hand-pumped petrol. It was here, too, that I first saw the most remarkable and indeed significant notice of the twentieth century; FREE AIR. When I made a habit of having my bicycle tyres replenished at this machine I did not grasp the delicate economic implications; but Henry, who never objected, understanding my innocence, was well on the way to affording all sorts of generosity. Sometimes he wore a suit at work and was cloistered in the little office. Then he was no longer Henry, but Mr. Williams. Very shortly after the move, he installed a Combine Harvester—the first in our area—on half the forecourt and hired it out to doubting farmers. They were converted. Behind the garage, in what had been long gardens running down to the river, the concrete spread.

In the beginning, however, while the paint on the garage was still fresh, I got some idea of how the transaction seemed to Bounce. I had walked round and round our tiny lawn, thinking and wishing. I had pushed between the fruit trees in the vegetable part and stood facing a corner of brick wall, in the place which always seemed most private to me. It was as if I had to come here to make a decision, here to this privacy where nothing but the spiders between the bricks could influence me—where I was not only away from people, but as nearly as possible away from the pressure of them. I had had a cloudy illumination. All my feelings had run together. The names of pianists were better known to me than the names of footballers. Here, I could wrestle with my sense of rank indecency at wanting to play the piano seriously, play it properly the way Myra Hess and Solomon did. Already I knew the delight of finding that my fingers could get round music I had thought impossible for them. Yet next year I should begin to work for a scholarship at Oxford. Physics and Chemistry were the real, the serious thing. The world, my parents implied, was my oyster, by way of Chemistry and Physics. I went from the angle of brick wall to Bounce's music room with a breath-taking purpose. I initiated a conversation! I talked about a career. I adopted the self-mocking tone I used when discussing anything with her that was important to me—a precaution that allowed me to leap on her side of the fence and treat the whole thing as a joke if she disapproved of it. Jeeringly then, I suggested that I might become a musician—a pianist, perhaps.

To my surprise, Bounce didn't laugh. She leaned back her head, drew the last thread of smoke in, then carefully stubbed the cigarette out. She kept her eyes solemnly on the keys.

"Your father would never agree."

Of course. Away from the angle of brick, and in cold daylight, his agreement was absolutely essential.

"Oh I don't know, Miss Dawlish—"

She was silent for a while.

"What does your mother think about it?"

All at once the *obscenity* of erratic, unpensioned music presented itself to me.

"Honestly, Miss Dawlish—I hadn't thought seriously about it—honestly, Miss Dawlish!"

Bounce folded her hands in her lap. When she spoke, there was a curious, flat bitterness in her voice that I had never heard there before.

"Don't be a musician, Kummer, my son. Go into the garage business if you want to make money. As for me, I shall have to slave at music till I drop down dead."

I nodded, soberly, servilely. Bounce swayed, and went off to sleep, her mouth making little chewing movements. Then her cheeks twisted, her mouth sucked in, and she jerked awake.

"That great boy still sleeping in the same room as his sister—it's disgusting! But you can't tell her. Can't tell her anything. What do they expect?"

A kind of personalized chill crept over my skin. I waited in the silence, glancing nervously at the brown photograph of the young man who stared perpetually past me—glanced from him to the brown photograph of the lady in cap and gown. But Bounce had seen my feet. She looked up and up, till her eyes reached my face. Suddenly there was recognition in them.

"It's old Kummer! What are you waiting for? Start playing!"

The next time I appeared with Mary's tonic, hoping against hope to get past the music room and into the yard without meeting Bounce, I went through the hall on tiptoe, opened the door into the yard and stepped straight into a family hurricane. Mary was defending the scullery doorway and facing Bounce. Henry had his back—very broad in an overcoat—had his back turned to me.

Bounce shouted suddenly.

"Well, I won't have him in my house!"

Henry was calm, but with both hands up to appease and quell.

"Look, Auntie Cis, Mary's got a headache—"

"And I don't have headaches, I suppose?"

"He's *my* boy, Jacky is, and I'll do what I like. He's none of your business!"

"Now Mary—don't speak to Auntie like that!"

"You'd better go, all of you. Go!"

Then they were aware of me. I went forward at last, shambling over the flagstones, and held out the bottle. Mary put back her fallen hair with one hand and took the bottle with the other.

"Kew."

I got away on my hot, adolescent feet as quickly as I could. But of course they did not go. A week later, and relations between Bounce and Mary were saccharine again. After that, there was another row, and so on; but still they did not go. Was it in some confusion of my dreams, or listening to her as she slept on the organ seat that I remember her moaning— "Oh Henry, Henry my dear! What's to become of me?"

My own musical future was decided with nothing but a token resistance from me. If I could not be a professional musician, at least I thought I might take a piano examination. When I braced myself and put this point to Bounce, she sat for a while, thinking, then laughed with a flash of gold teeth.

"Be careful, Kummer—be very careful!"

"Well. I really want to, Miss Dawlish."

Bounce shook on the organ seat.

"You're not too highly strung?"

"I want to take an ARCM."

"What does your father say?"

"He's willing—provided it doesn't interfere with my work of course."

"We'd have to start from the beginning. You've just been picking about at the piano, haven't you?"

"Yes, Miss Dawlish."

Bounce turned to the keyboard. She pulled a dusty and dog-eared volume out of the mess on the piano, flicked over the pages, arranged them on the music rest then began to play. When she had finished she lit a cigarette.

"There you are. Now you know what you're up against."

I hope she took my mutter for awe. But the truth is that I was stunned. What she had played was a Chopin Impromptu. The night before I had heard Cortot play it.

"I'll work hard."

"You'll have to. There'll be theory too. And ear tests. We haven't tested your ear out for a long time, have we? Not since you were—*that* high. Turn round, Kummer."

I turned away from the piano and faced the yellowing

195

muslin curtains. She began to strike intervals, then groups of more and more complex dissonance. In my mind's eye, I saw where she put down each thick finger. It was like reading very large print. She finished, and I turned round.

Then she said a curious thing.

"Your father must be proud of you."

I had no answer to this. Presently she began to talk.

"My father took endless trouble over ear tests. If I couldn't pick the middle note out of—say—that lot, Crack! would go his ruler over my knuckles—"

She was staring towards the wall, so I looked the same way. I saw the faded sepia photograph of the young man who had hung all those years by the lady in cap and gown, as overseer of the music room. So great was the shock that I did not hear what Bounce was saying. For I had suddenly recognized the hairless eyes and brows, the high cheekbones. The young man—I saw now that he was hardly older than I—was old Mr. Dawlish, his hair flying, his eye already fixed on the absolute.

"—very cold sometimes in the morning. But he knew what it was about. He'd say 'You go on practising, my girl. That'll warm you'. Still, heaven is music, isn't it, Kummer?"

"Yes, Miss Dawlish."

So now there began a time for me of peace and delight, in which the sky over Stilbourne lifted to infinite distance. Music, music, music, all no longer shady, obscene, but wholly legal—what everybody agreed I ought to be doing. Now the quarrels in the old house were an irritation rather than a way of passing some of my lessons. I would stand restlessly in the hall, wondering where Bounce had got to, and whether I should get my full thirty minutes. Then I would hear her furious voice from the yard.

"Then why don't you go? Go!"

Their crazy relationship staggered on, Henry holding some

sort of balance, understanding both parties and battered from both directions. Then Bounce would come into the music room, her vast bosom heaving, and I would have what was left of the lesson. Nevertheless, the end of music was nearer than I supposed. I had battered too long and too devotedly at our ancient piano. As the disapproving remarks came in from the chemistry and physics masters who had once been so pleased with me, my parents took notice.

"Well I know you've got a piano lesson tomorrow; but you've also got a chemistry lesson tomorrow!"

"Look—Father. Didn't you learn the violin?"

"I never let it come between me and the *Materia Medica*— Oliver, don't you really *want* to go to Oxford?"

" 'Course I do."

"These last months are so important, dear," said my mother pleadingly. "You know we only want what's best for you."

The old shame, inculcated year after year, at the idea of becoming a professional musician kept me silent. As if he was reading my mind, my father peered kindly at me across the table. If he had been angry, I could have withstood him; but he sounded understanding and sympathetic as if we were both face to face with iron necessity.

"You'll have to keep it as a hobby, the way I did. Anyway the gramophone and wireless are going to put most professional musicians out of business. Good Lord, Oliver, don't you understand? With opportunities like yours, you might even become a *doctor*!"

So then I had the difficulty of confessing to Bounce that I was not going to work for my ARCM after all; but she said little, merely nodding as if she had expected this. Our lessons returned to the old way of wasting time. Indeed, we wasted more time than before, since the rows had reached a critical point. Henry might escape from the hall, gently but firmly, secure in his brown, double-breasted suit with the two fountain pens in the breast pocket, but he would leave flames behind him.

"And you don't owe me *anything*, I suppose!"

"We've given as much as we've took!"

And still they did not go.

"I won't have him here, that horrible, *horrible* boy—he was torturing it—"

My last lesson came and went; and after a restless summer, I reached the excitement and tremor of packing for Oxford. It was only on the evening before I went that I thought of Bounce again, because of the large square van parked on the cobbles in front of her railings.

"What's up with Bounce, Mother?"

My mother jerked her head in contempt.

"They've gone."

"Who?"

"The Williams's. Who d'you think? The Pope?" She made a noise as near as nothing to a spit. "I knew they would, one day when she was no more use to him. They've taken one of the new bungalows for the time being. It's said that Henry Williams is going to build himself a house. I never trusted the man. Never."

I could not remember that my mother had ever had any dealings with Henry, and I wondered how she could be so definite. I watched the door of the house open, and men bring out a few sticks of furniture, carpets, rugs, crockery and beds. My mother watched at my side.

"All shoddy, second-hand stuff. Never spent a penny he didn't have to."

Presently the van drew away and my mother returned to her sewing. A pupil, complete with music, went in at Bounce's door.

"You'd better go over this evening after she's finished teaching and say goodbye to her," said my mother. "You owe her that."

"Oh no! Look—Mother!"

"Nonsense," said my mother calmly. "You know you're devoted to her."

So that evening, when the sodium lamps had shuddered into their ghastly brightness round the Square, I went, a young man dripping with hair oil and burning to get away, across the grass to the old house. The bow window was dark, and I hoped deeply that she was out, or asleep; for the guessed-at lights of Oxford, the concerts and plays, the books and people that would be mine in the intervals of chemistry, drew me strongly, and I could not think of anything else. But looking back at our cottage, I saw how a corner of the curtain was lifted to leave a little triangle in which I felt my mother's eye. So sighing deeply, I stepped over the chains and onto the cobbles. I opened her front door; and the cold thought fell on me that once more the corridor and the rooms upstairs were dark and empty. Even that hall was haunted again; and despite my eighteen years I left the front door open as a retreat. Sodium light from the Square outlined a window on the floor and lay vertically against the door of the music room. With a tightening of the chest—and perhaps with the phantom of a quarter-size violin in my left hand—I raised the other hand to knock; and took it back again.

The sounds that came from beyond the dark panelling were a kind of ear-test. But a rook had no business to be down there on the left, on the rug before the dull, red eye of the fire. Nor could it add to its faint cawing those curious, strangled sounds as from an incompetently handled instrument. I stood stone-still left hand down, right hand raised, and listened as the caws and chokes prolonged and multiplied themselves; and the ear-test provided the picture I could see as clearly as if no panelling divided us. She was down there in the dark on the left, huddled before the dim fire beneath the glowering bust; trying to learn unsuccessfully without a teacher, how to sob her heart out.

I stole away, my hair lifting against the oil. I closed the door as carefully as if I had committed a burglary. I hastened across the grass and tried to sneak upstairs without my mother seeing me. But though she was sewing still, she had kept her ears open.

"Didn't have a long talk then, Oliver?"

I grunted, as much like my father as I could.

"Come in and tell me about it."

Groaning, and curiously enough, blushing as if I had been detected in some impropriety, I went into the sitting room.

"What did she have to say, dear?"

"—She wasn't there."

"Nonsense! She hasn't left the house."

"She wasn't there I tell you! Perhaps she's gone to bed."

My mother looked up at me over her spectacles and smiled slightly.

"Perhaps she has."

I went away from Stilbourne then, thinking this was my final escape. But I might have known that as long as I was connected with it in any way, we should all continue, even at a distance, to exercise some kind of gravitational influence over each other. Thus, the first copy of the *Stilbourne Advertiser* which my mother forwarded to me contained not only news of my grand elevation to the status of undergraduate, but also news of Bounce. I read how Miss C. C. Dawlish (well-known local resident) had been involved in an accident at the junction between Cold Harbour Lane and the King's Path. Little damage had been done but Miss Dawlish had sustained shock. This seemed not very significant to me; but

I learned better in the Easter Vacation when I went home. I was spending as much time as I could, walking in the countryside. I had gone down across the Old Bridge, walked up the hill on the other side of the valley and was as far as I could be from the Square. I was brooding on the cheapest way of spending the Long Vacation abroad, somewhere; so it was not surprising that I almost walked into her. The two seater was at right-angles to the road. It had crossed the grass verge and the front wheels were in a muddy ditch. Bounce stood by it, gazing impassively into the woods. I had no chance of avoiding her.

"Hullo, Miss Dawlish! Having trouble?"

Her eyes turned first, then her head. Her mouth was very tight, the deep grooves running into it.

"You're not hurt, Miss Dawlish, are you?"

All at once her face relaxed and lightened.

"It's old Kummer!"

"Can't I help?"

"Help?"

The darkness and tightness settled on her face again. The grooves came back. She began to shake her head, slowly and solemnly.

"No. No, no, no."

"I could push——"

"No. No."

A milk lorry came bumping and rattling along through the woods.

"Shall I—"

"No."

She had not stopped shaking her head. She was frowning and saying "No" as if faced by some very difficult problem, the answer to which was only just out of reach.

"Well then—"

Suddenly the darkness lifted. It was extraordinary and

frightening; there was such an instantaneity about the change—like a wireless with a dud valve when the sound is here one moment then clicks away into the distance. Her eyes focused on me, she grinned and showed her gold teeth.

"It's old Kummer! Are you looking for a girl in the woods?"

I remembered the whole business of Evie Babbacombe and I felt my face blaze. I backed away, holding my walking stick like a sword.

"I—"

"How's the piano then, my son?"

"No."

"Better things to do, eh?"

I felt the sweat on my forehead.

"Chemistry and Physics, nowadays. Look—I'm walking back into Stilbourne. It'll take a long time, I'm afraid. I'll try to get a lift. Shall I fetch Henry?"

She put back her head and laughed.

"Do you know, Kummer? He always services my car himself—changes the oil and all those things, things inside, I don't know what they are. And he always cleans it himself, washes it, polishes it. He puts on overalls and gets down to it just like he—"

"I'll fetch him, Miss Dawlish. You're quite sure you don't want me to stay? You'll be all right, here in the—?"

"Here in the woods?'

She laughed again. Then the darkness and tightness was back, eyes unblinking.

"I'm quite safe. Nobody's going to bother about an old lady like me. Quite safe."

"I'll be as quick as I can."

I hurried along the track, taking the shortest way to Stilbourne. I turned before I reached the corner and waved, as if to assure her of something or other, but she never saw me.

She was standing on the verge by the car, staring into the woods. I came to a long bend in the road and there, a hundred yards away, was Henry's breakdown van approaching. I shouted and gesticulated back to Bounce, trying to convey this to her by a kind of incompetent semaphore. I shouted and pointed at the van, too; but Henry passed me without noticing, in his brown double-breasted suit and trilby hat—passed me, staring mournfully before him through the windscreen. I waited, until I saw his van draw up beside her.

At supper, when I was questioned about my walk, my mother was very interested. She listened to my factual account of my meeting with Bounce, nodding and smiling grimly. My father looked up at her over his spectacles.

"Getting worse."

I looked from one to the other.

"Worse? How? What's happened?"

My mother waved away my question.

"I knew how it would end when he'd got what he wanted."

"Come now," said my father ponderously, as he helped himself to more cottage pie, "Come now. She'll not have lost. She got her money back ten times over. I'll say that about young Williams. He's made a success of things."

"Not like some people I could mention," said my mother tartly. "By the time he's done, he'll have bought up half the town!"

I took this as a veiled allusion to the dull result of my first chemistry examination, so I kept quiet. My father kept quiet too. My mother had the air to herself: but she was used to this.

"Jacky Williams won't go to Oxford, not even if he has the brains, which I doubt. You'll see. He'll go straight into the business. That's how they'll go on. He could afford to send

203

him, but he won't. And poor Miss Dawlish, slaving away—"

But this was too much for my father.

"She's no need to," he said gruffly. "Why, with what she gets from the money she put into his business she could live like a—she could live in Bournemouth if she wanted to."

I was getting bored.

"Well, she was lucky this afternoon anyway. Let's leave it at that. Though I do think the milk lorry might have stopped."

"Lucky?" said my father. "Lucky?"

My mother echoed him.

"Lucky?"

They looked at each other then back at me.

"I mean she could have been stuck there. It took me an hour to get home. If Henry hadn't been coming through the woods—What's the matter?"

They had turned back to each other, my mother with a look of incredulous amusement.

"Oliver, dear," said my mother fondly. "You really *are*— but then, of course you've been away. Everybody knows about her—even the man in the milk lorry. She was a hundred yards from the cross roads in the woods, wasn't she?"

"Telephone box," said my father briefly. "She rang him up."

I shoved back my chair.

"My God! So there is!"

"Not luck at all."

"But she might have told me! I mean—there was I prepared to—"

My mother laughed aloud; then subsided.

"Poor soul!" she said. "All she wants is for him to put a little attention about her."

There was a sort of convulsion in my mind. Late, later than for anyone else in that neighbourhood, the pieces—

ancient and new—flew together, and I understood. My mouth opened and stayed open; for I had nothing to say. Yet they must have seen something in my frozen face, for my father put out a hand, clumsily, and laid it on my sleeve.

"We were forgetting how much she means to you, Oliver. But you see, old son—these telephone boxes—she's done it before."

My father's gesture was so unusual in our undemonstrative household that I grimaced and stood up. I muttered.

"Well, if she's got enough money—"

"Ah," said my mother darkly. "Money isn't everything. You'll find that out one day, Oliver."

I took my astonishment away; and in all that confusion of thought and feeling, I had a hazy awareness that the end of my mother's conversation had contradicted something in the earlier part of it; so that this was the first time I understood she was not only my mother. She was a woman. This mental revolution was emotional too and very confusing. I stood there in the hall, gloves on, scarf hanging down over chest and back, and was consumed with humiliation, resentment and a sort of stage fright, to think how we were all known, all food for each other, all clothed and ashamed in our clothing. I opened the front door to escape her understanding; but as I closed it I heard her burst out with a half-suppressed giggle—

"I wonder what she'll do when she runs out of 'phone boxes?"

So now when my mother sent me the *Stilbourne Advertiser* I searched it diligently. Sure enough, I learned not only that at the organ was Miss C. C. Dawlish, but on another page, how Miss C. C. Dawlish had been fined five pounds; and later still ten pounds. When I was at home during the vacations, I sometimes saw her—but from as far away as possible— pacing from the garage to the house, with the ghost of that old, elastic stride. I saw the darkness in her face, too, the ring of muscle contracted round her mouth, eyes unwinking.

"Poor soul," my mother would murmur mechanically. I think she had lost interest. Bounce was like the long-dead Ophelia with her hatful of leaves—a Stilbourne eccentric, assimilated and accepted. At last, I read how Miss C. C. Dawlish was the defendant, up for dangerous driving. She had hurt, not herself, but someone else. I read how the chairman of the bench had said that he accepted this and that; but that we were none of us getting any younger and it would be in Miss Dawlish's own interest, etcetera. He would suspend her licence for five years.

I read that, sitting in the window of my rooms with the spire of the university church stretching above me; and I remember how amused and cynical I was. Had she, indeed, reached the end of the available telephone boxes? Was this the next step? If so, she had been too clever by half. She had called attention to herself for the last time, I said to myself in my innocence. For I was a chemist, not a biologist. It was only when I was getting ready to return to Oxford for my last year, that I learned better.

That autumn was hot, and for once we had an Indian Summer. The hollyhocks were burning up where they stood. Either side of our front door they were dark brown sticks with a last flame of red or yellow at the tip. The grass plot in the Square was almost as brown as the stems and the individual blades snapped if you stepped on them. I could hear my mother moving about in the kitchen, getting things together for supper; but there was no other noise in the house. My father had not yet finished in the dispensary so that I had our little sitting room to myself. I could hear Bounce practising in the church—a voluntary of impeccable dullness. I stood, among our chintz and china, listening and watching. Then the organ stopped and shortly afterwards I saw Bounce walk quickly along the other side of the Square and go into her house. I was glad she was securely tucked away because it meant there was no chance of my meeting her. The Square was deserted. It was safe to go out.

The door of Bounce's house opened. She came out, walking as ever very upright. Her flat, corduroy hat was skewered to her thinning hair. She pulled the door to behind her and put on her gloves without looking at them. Her face was calm and smiling. She turned left and paced along the pavement towards Henry's garage. She looked neither to right nor left. The air was so still I could hear the tap tap of her shoes on the flat stones. I watched her till she passed beyond the Town Hall and disappeared.

I found myself writhing, twisting, sneaking on hurried feet—but nevertheless slamming into the sitting room door—sliding back, past the kitchen, past the scullery, out into the garden, down between the fruit trees—then back in my brick angle and alone; but staring, staring—trying to find something on which I might fasten my eye and blind my mind's eye. There was a storm in me which felt as if it were around me, so that the dry webs of spiders between the bricks seemed part of it and of her and me, and everything. I could hear my own voice as if someone else was using it.

"No. No. Oh-No. No. No—"

And I knew even then that the sight was seared into me, branded where I lived, ineradicable—Bounce pacing along the pavement with her massive bosom, thick stomach and rolling, ungainly haunches; Bounce wearing her calm smile, her hat and gloves and flat shoes—and wearing nothing else whatsoever.

After that, Bounce vanished. The house was the same, and her two seater still stood on Henry's premises—still washed and polished. Nobody mentioned Bounce. She had become one of those cases on which Stilbourne turned its corporate back. Indeed I should never have had any certain knowledge of what happened to her in all those years had I not deliberately—shamelessly—raised the question. It was during the last of my parents' yearly visits to me at Oxford. It was after tea, during the lame hour we spent between that ceremony and the train's departure. I had come, as I always did—glad though I was to see them—had come to the point of silence, when none of us could think what to say next. We looked at each other now across a kind of gulf of years and differing experience. Only the embarrassment of such a painful silence could have induced me to broach the topic.

"By the way, how's Bounce, Mother? I didn't see her at all last time."

The silence was intense again. My father busied himself with filling his pipe, and kept his pebble glasses very close to it.

"She was ill," said my mother with delicate enunciation "—you know. She had to go away."

Their glances flickered to and from each other.

"It was a bad business," said my father, fumbling with matches. "A very bad business."

My mother patted her mouth with a lace handkerchief.

"Poor soul," she said.

The silence lengthened and deepened. So that was that.

Nevertheless I was to meet Bounce again, though not for many years. The war came on us and the peace; and after years of peace I went back with my family to persuade my mother she must not live alone in the cottage but make her home with us. Yet neither I nor my wife could cope with her mixture of tears and hysteria. I felt it was very bad for the children and I tried to calm her.

"It's cats," said my mother, wiping her eyes, "You know I can't stand cats."

"Well, never mind—"

"But I *do* mind. She ought to be told. She's got so many of them, she's out half the night, 'Puss, puss, come to Mummie den! Milkies—' I simply can't sleep—"

"Who's got so many cats, Mother?"

"She has. Miss Dawlish," said my mother angrily. "I haven't any patience with the woman."

"Bounce!"

"You must go and tell her about them, Oliver. I won't have it!"

"Bounce! She's back? I thought—I thought she was—"

"Of course she's back. Been back a long time. You must tell her, Oliver!"

"But we shall all be gone in a few—"

My mother burst into a storm of tears.

"Well you must speak to her! And your father not cold in his—The place is swarming with them! Suppose they got in here!"

I patted her shoulder, with a clumsy gesture so like my father's that I took it away hurriedly.

"All right, Mother. I'll go across and see her, anyway."

"Besides. You were always so—"

"I know, Mother, dear. I'm devoted to her."

I went out and stood in the Square, bracing myself. Mark was machine-gunning Sophy who was ignoring him and throwing daisies about; but when they saw me they came running. I took one in each hand and went across to the door by the bow window. It was open, so we went in and stood for a while in the hall. I knocked on the music room door and got no answer; but the door down into the yard was open too. We went through, I, at least, glad to be out in the open air; for cats and canaries and budgerigars had added to the already stale house an entirely new dimension of fetor. As I stepped down, an evil-looking Tom slid by us into the

209

house, and two seconds later I heard the spats and hisses and the furry thumps of a fight.

Bounce was coming slowly up the garden path, seeming broader than it, square. The corduroy hat was still skewered to her hair, and her tie divided an enormous expanse. She stopped, two yards away, and examined the three of us.

"Hullo, Miss Dawlish. Do you remember me?"

"It's old Kummer. Are these yours?"

"This is Mark and this is Sophy. How are you, Miss Dawlish?"

"Let's go inside."

She led the way into the hall. We followed, the children pressing close to me. I began to have an uneasy feeling that perhaps this was not so good an idea after all. Bounce peered at a budgerigar which ignored her and went on contemplating its own entrancing reflection in a little mirror. She made noises at it.

"Weep, weep, weep!"

"Mark—for God's sake, child! Not in public! Here— you'd better run along home."

Bounce watched him out of the door.

"That boy of his did very well in the war. You can never tell, can you?"

"I suppose not."

"What did you do, Kummer?"

I thought back.

"I enjoyed a very peaceful war, I'm afraid. We had to have gas ready, of course. But we never used it."

She turned back to the budgerigar.

"Weep, weep!"

"You've got very fond of animals, haven't you?"

"I always was, even when I was—as small as your daughter. Do you know, Kummer? I used to pretend I was a boy so that I could pretend I was a vet! But of course with my music

I didn't have time for pets. Then afterwards, with that horrible boy in the house, I couldn't possibly have them."

I realized with a shock, how time was foreshortening for her. But before I could say anything more she went on. Her eyes had a kind of insolence in them.

"I was ill for a long time," she said. "Seriously ill. You knew, didn't you?"

I became a small boy again with a quarter-size violin. Wordlessly, I shook my head. Suddenly her slablike cheeks broke up, gold teeth flashed, and she roared with laughter.

"But I'm better now—much, much better!"

I felt my daughter's cheek press against the back of my hand; but Bounce stopped laughing, bent down, and spoke severely to a pair of ferocious eyes that blazed in the darkness under the stairs.

"Naughty! Naughty!"

The Tom slid past us and out at the front door. Bounce straightened up.

"Would you believe it?" she said. "He's as much trouble as a child. He keeps me up, waiting to open the door, all hours of the night!"

"Do what Isaac Newton did for his cats. He cut holes with flaps in the door for them—a big hole for the big cat and a little hole for the little cat."

After a few seconds the joke hit Bounce. She rocked and roared.

"And then you wouldn't have to bother to let him in."

Bounce stopped laughing.

"Henry would do it," she said. "He'd make the hole properly. I'll ask Henry. He would come up and do it or bring one of His Men with him."

I nodded, moving towards the door.

"Well then—"

"Do you know he still polishes my car? In overalls. No one

else touches it." She nodded meaningly to me. "It's a penance you see. And that woman—she's another penance. Henry understands. He always understands, doesn't he?"

"Yes. Yes, he does."

"But as for other people—" She looked at the music room door, then down at Sophy. "Has your daughter started to play yet?"

"She's not started yet. But she's very fond of music, aren't you, Sophy?"

My daughter nuzzled into my trouser leg, away from the square woman with the slablike cheeks. I put my hand through her hair, feeling the fragility of her head and neck; and a great surge of love came over me, protection, compassion, and the fierce determination that she should never know such lost solemnity but be a fulfilled woman, a wife and mother.

"I used to call your father 'Kummer' because he was always late."

I shifted my feet.

"Well. I suppose we must—"

"Goodbye, then, Kummer."

"After all these years, I ought to thank—"

"Don't bother. It doesn't mean anything, does it?"

She turned towards the yard; then stopped and looked at me.

"D'you know, Kummer? If I could save a child or a budgie from a burning house, I'd save the budgie."

"I—"

"Goodbye. I don't suppose we shall meet again."

She went heavily down the two steps and I heard her flat shoes pacing through the yard.

Never again.

The ton of marble, the harp, the stone chips, the *immor-*

telles, white marble surround, the organ thundering out from the south transept—

CLARA CECILIA DAWLISH
1890—1960

—and amid the thunder of the organ, the three words in smaller letters, written almost between my feet:

Heaven is Music

I caught myself up, appalled at my wanton laughter in that place; and as if a long finger had reached out and touched me, I felt in every nerve that my shudders came out of the ground itself. For it was here, close and real, two yards away as ever, that pathetic, horrible, unused body, with the stained frills and Chinese face. This was a kind of psychic ear-test before which nothing survived but revulsion and horror, childishness and atavism, as if unnameable things were rising round me and blackening the sun. I heard my own voice—as if it could make its own bid for honesty—crying aloud.

"I never liked you! Never!"

Then I was outside the churchyard, standing on the grass in the centre of the Square; and for that moment I could not think how I had got there. A middle-aged man, running away as though he had found himself once more in the long corridor between the empty rooms!

A girl laughed with a high tinkle from the window of the Wilsons's house, which now bore the sign EMPLOYMENT EXCHANGE. An icecream van bumped past my father's cottage, calling attention to itself with a vibraphone. Beyond the pillars of the Town Hall, I could see twelve white television figures serve twelve identical aces. The gooseflesh lay down on me by degrees; and from the security of my own warm life, I set myself to speak, inside myself, of how things were.

I was afraid of you, and so I hated you. It is as simple as that. When I heard you were dead I was glad.

I walked forward towards her house. The front door was not merely open, but off the hinges and leaning against the wall. There was a neat, square hole in the bottom panel, closed by a springloaded flap. The workmen had made a chalky tangle of bootmarks between the front door and the steps down to the yard. I went to the music room, lifted my hand to knock, then remembered. I flung the door open so that it crashed back then rebounded from the panelled wall. Instantly with the crash, there came a fierce, papery beating from the window beyond the muslin curtains—or from beyond where the curtains had been. I stood stock still, hands up. The thing beat mindlessly with frayed wings among the cobwebs on the pane. I ran forward to wrestle with the sash; but the maimed thing fluttered down to the floor and lay there motionless. The keyboard hung there, invisibly present in the empty room, the row of organ pedals lay just above a square of unworn floor boarding. My eye put back two brown photographs on their squares of lighter panelling. I had had all I wanted of the music room.

I paused in the hall, envisaging the long corridor at the head of the stairs. But no. There was a limit to exorcism. I went quickly down the two steps, through the yard into the garden, and blessed the warm hand of the sun.

Henry's men had already begun to dismantle the long wall that lay between the laurel bushes, the laburnum trees, and his spreading business. They had piled the valuable old brick; but in two places the wall had collapsed under its own weight, hiding flowers and weeds under a pile of red clay and yellow cement. I was curious to see the bottom of the garden where I had never been; and I walked forward along a cinder path that plantains and dandelions had invaded. I pushed between laurels, and the little river was before me. This end of the garden was an enclosure by the river bank, with stone steps, forget-me-nots, wallflowers not yet in blossom, and shallow, sliding water. On the top step above the water, was a windsor chair. Though spiders had spun between the members, and birds had fouled the seat; though the polish had cracked into a dark roughness, yet the chair stood there, mutely insisting how she had used it—every evening perhaps, in the last summer and autumn, among the midges and swifts. Opposite the chair and against the long wall, was a surround of brick; and the wall above it was black with smoke. I peered into the surround, and saw at once that this had been no ordinary bonfire. Even after the rain of two or more winters, there were still enough bits and pieces, spines, corners, whole sodden covers indeed, for me to decipher them. *Breitkopf Und Hartel, Augener, MacMillan, Boosey and Hawkes,* and the almost incombustible stacks of the *Musical Times*—

Henry could never have done it. The music had been worth real money. I saw a glint of metal, picked out a steel strip and my guess became certainty. The lead bob had melted away, but the knife-edge and the sliding weight that adjusted the ticking of the metronome to an unbearable accuracy were identifiable. Henry would never have burnt old Mr. Dawlish's metronome, that valuable antique, in its polished case. Nor, I thought, as I caught a bleak eye staring at me from the ground, would he have smashed Beethoven into plaster fragments with a hammer blow. And that sodden angle of wood, might well be all that was left of a frame and a photograph—

I sat on her chair, put my elbows on my knees and my face

in my hands. I did not know to what or whom my feelings had reference, nor even what they were.

"You've looked all over, then?"

Henry stood on the other side of the gap in the wall, brown face, liquid eyes, white hair—all very trim and calm. I got up and began to climb the pile of bricks, clumsily.

"Can I lend you a hand?"

"I can manage by myself—thanks."

Side by side, we sauntered back between the machines. Our heads were bowed, hands clasped behind us, pace very slow, like mourners.

"That was a nice thought of yours, Henry, that inscription."

He said nothing. I glanced sideways at him.

"Quick to feel, slow to learn. That's me."

We stopped and faced each other.

"You could say, Henry—you *could* say—"

You could say that the only time she was ever calm and happy, with a relaxed, smiling face, they put her away until she was properly cured and unhappy again. You could say that, for example.

But really, you could say nothing.

"It doesn't matter."

"We walked on again in silence to the pavement before the apron. I took out some notes to pay for the petrol and looked for the Petrol Lady. She emerged, but Henry waved her away.

"Allow me, sir. No, not at all. It's a pleasure, meeting you after all these years."

He took my money and went to change it. I stood, looking down at the worn pavement, so minutely and illegibly inscribed; and I saw the feet, my own among them, pass and repass. I stretched out a leg and tapped with my live toe,

216

listening meanwhile, tap, tap, tap—and suddenly I felt that if I might only lend my own sound, my own flesh, my own power of choosing the future, to those invisible feet, I would pay anything—*anything*: but knew in the same instant that, like Henry, I would never pay more than a reasonable price.

"—and ninepence is three pounds. Thank you, sir."

I looked him in the eye; and saw my own face.

"Goodbye, Henry."

He raised his hand, saying nothing. I got into my car of superior description, moved away, over the Old Bridge and at last on to the motor road. I concentrated resolutely on my driving.